WORDSWORTH CLASSICS
OF WORLD LITERATURE

General Editor: Tom Griffith MA, MPhil

SATYRICON

Petronius
Satyricon

❖

Translated by Paul Dinnage
With an Introduction and Notes
by Costas Panayotakis

WORDSWORTH CLASSICS
OF WORLD LITERATURE

This edition published 1999 by Wordsworth Editions Limited
Cumberland House, Crib Street, Ware, Hertfordshire SG12 9ET

ISBN 1 84022 110 0

Typeset by Antony Gray
Printed and bound in Great Britain by
Mackays of Chatham, Chatham, Kent

CONTENTS

INTRODUCTION

Unlike the only other surviving genuinely Roman novel, Apuleius' *The Golden Ass,* the *Satyricon is* a frustratingly enigmatic text, since all scholarly theories concerning its author and date of composition, its original length and mode of delivery, its generic identity and literary originality, and (most importantly) its purpose may be refuted by the discovery of its beginning, its ending, or a substantial section of its main body.

The surviving *Satyricon* contains substantial fragments from apparently 'Books fourteen, fifteen, and sixteen' of the original work; we do not know exactly how much more there was. It recounts, in an elegant first-person prose narrative interspersed with poems of various length, the adventures of the comic rogue Encolpius and his occasional companions as they travel around the bay of Naples in search of a free meal and a pleasurable life. Encolpius ('Mr Groin') is a bisexual anti-hero suffering from impotence; his companions are the pretty slave boy and Encolpius' unfaithful concubine Giton ('Neighbour'), and the formidable and admirably well-endowed ex-lover of Encolpius Ascyltus ('Mr Indefatigable').

Their satirically and theatrically coloured encounters with the hypocritical teacher of rhetoric Agamemnon, the orgiastic priestess of the phallic god Priapus Quartilla, the eccentrically vulgar and excessively wealthy freedman Trimalchio, the old and lecherous poetaster Eumolpus, the superstitious captain Lichas, the seductive lady Tryphaena, the beautiful nymphomaniac matron Circe, the bibulous ancient witches Proselenus and Oenothea, and the unscrupulous legacy-huntress Philomela enable the author to satirise social, religious, and cultural issues of his time, and to invoke a host of widely differing literary genres (Greek romantic fiction, epic, elegy, oratory, historiography, to name but a few), only to subvert them for his learned audience's amusement.

The dense literary texture of the *Satyricon,* however, does not suggest that it is a disorderly gathering of various elements from different literary genres; there is nothing remotely similar to the *Satyricon* in the extant Greek and Roman literature, and its originality lies not so much in its obscene plot or its literary ingredients but in the sophisticated way literary tradition and real life are first refashioned and then blended to create an uncompromising work, which refuses to be pigeonholed. Who is responsible for this anarchic text?

Most scholars nowadays concur with the generally accepted view that the mysterious author of this novel, whose name appears in most manuscripts as 'Petronius Arbiter', is Emperor Nero's courtier Titus Petronius Niger, consul in AD 62 and Nero's 'Tutor in Refinement' (*Elegantiae Arbiter*). If we are right in identifying the creator of Encolpius' fictional adventures with the man who, by AD 63, was responsible for the evaluation of both cultural and aesthetic matters in Nero's court, we are fortunate enough to possess a concise depiction of his character, including a fascinating account of his last moments, by Tacitus (*Annals* 16.18 ff.). The Roman historiographer, who disapproved of (but was also clearly intrigued by) Petronius' eccentrically luxurious life-style, portrays Petronius as a charmingly unconventional man, who is the personification of cynicism in all its glory. From being a proconsul in the Roman province of Bithynia he had managed to become Nero's trusted friend and the central cultural figure in the Imperial court, but showed no signs of fear or distress when he realised that he had lost his former power and fallen victim to the envy of his rivals, who accused him of treason. Consequently, he was forced to commit suicide.

We are told that Petronius opened his veins and bound them up or reopened them, that he listened to light verse, that he flogged some slaves and rewarded others, that he ate and slept, and that he even wrote an account of Nero's perverse sexual activities, which he then sent to the Emperor himself; the frivolity with which he chose to face death subverts deliberately and masterfully the details of the dictated suicide of the worthy Stoic philosopher and tragedian Seneca, Petronius' predecessor as the central cultural figure in

Nero's palace, who was also both accused of conspiring against his former pupil, Nero, and required to put an end to his life. Unlike Petronius, however, Seneca chose a peaceful and moving end, which in turn was meant to mirror the dignified death of the wise Athenian philosopher Socrates.

It seems quite plausible to argue that Petronius, whose life and death were not governed by 'real wisdom' or 'reason', the principles of Stoic philosophy, would also have opted to exercise his literary talents on a kind of literature which was both diametrically opposed to Seneca's literary tastes, and scarcely a highly respected occupation for educated and serious-minded Roman aristocrats. The *Satyricon* is perhaps best seen, then, as a consciously risible successor to Seneca's moral tragedies, which, unlike Encolpius' hedonistic and dangerous adventures in the gutter of an already declining Rome, dealt with the sufferings of kings and queens, heroes and heroines, who had crossed the boundaries of 'reason' and 'nature' in the remote temporal and spatial sphere of Greek mythology.

Equally strong, however, in Tacitus' account is the impression that Petronius treated his death as a spectacle, which he himself staged, in order to transform what at the time seemed to be an unavoidable suicide into a natural and everlasting sleep; it is not coincidental, I believe, that a recurrent motif in the plot of the *Satyricon* is the idea of life being a series of well-rehearsed theatrical postures, that the sub-literary genre of the Roman mime has exerted such a great influence on Petronius that the principal characters of the novel are constantly involved in role-playing, and that two of them, the vulgar millionaire Trimalchio and the mediocre poet Eumolpus, are also shown to stage their death-scenes in an equally frivolous manner, with some piquant similarities to specific details in Tacitus' passage.

The *Satyricon* is not mentioned by contemporaries or near-contemporaries of Petronius, and its date of composition cannot be proved beyond any doubt. Nevertheless, no convincing argument has been put forth so far against the well-argued case that Petronius wrote the *Satyricon* within a period of two or three years before the summer of AD 66, the date of his dictated suicide. I do not believe that Petronius' intended audience was the wide public, and I am inclined to accept the view that this novel was read aloud in instalments, either by Petronius or by an educated slave, to a small, selected circle of the author's learned and trusted friends. On the other hand, the case for solitary reading and private enjoyment of the text cannot be ruled out.

The surviving *Satyricon* has rightly been characterised by Niall Slater as 'a scholarly embarrassment' in the sense that, although it bears many resemblances to various literary genres – such as the sentimental Greek romances or the moralising Menippean satire, which, like the *Satyricon,* combined prose and verse in its narrative – it cannot be unanimously classified as an example of any one of them. It is conventionally regarded as a 'comic-realistic novel', an inadequate term because, among other reasons, this label did not exist in antiquity, and is used also for Apuleius' fictional work, in spite of the striking differences between that novel and the *Satyricon.* Although modern critics have not given up trying to decode the generic identity of this text (Gareth Schmeling's very attractive theory that the *Satyricon* should be regarded as the 'confession' of the pompous and unreliable narrator Encolpius is the most recent view on this difficult issue), it is important to note that the generic label mentioned above effectively distinguishes the *Satyricon* from Greek romantic texts, which existed already in the first century BC, and portrayed the highly moral love of idealised heterosexual protagonists struggling to overcome Fortune's obstacles in order to attain a lifelong happy union.

In fact, Petronius' debt to the Greek novelistic tradition is clearly indicated already in the cleverly chosen title of his work, *Satyricon,* which is most likely the Latin transliteration of the Greek word Σατυρικῶν (neuter genitive plural of the adjective σατυρικός meaning 'related to satyrs', the lewd followers of Bacchus), and should be understood as an adjective depending on the Latin noun 'libri'; thus the complete title of the novel would mean 'books of lascivious events', and would hint at the kind of story presented by the author. But this conventional function of the title, whose form resembles the form of the titles of several other Greek romances (for example, *A Pastoral Story, An Ephesian Story, An Ethiopian Story*), would also indicate to Petronius' audience that, in composing his story, he was exploiting the characters, the plot elements, the episodic narrative structure and (possibly) the combination of prose and verse, of popular Greek romantic fiction.

Moreover, although there is no etymological connection between the title of Petronius' novel and the Latin word *satura*, used to denote the literary genre of Roman satire, it is sensible to argue that the acoustic similarity of these two words would invite Petronius' audience to view at least some of the characters and events of the novel's plot in a satirical light, where the biting humour is directed not only against highly regarded literary genres such as epic and historiography, or well-established social and religious institutions such as inheritance and the cult of Priapus, or traditional Roman values such as female chastity and loyalty to one's friends, or distinguished persons of the author's lifetime, including perhaps Nero, but also against Encolpius himself. This is a great source of comic effect in the novel.

A summary of the surviving text demonstrates clearly its episodic structure, an element which Petronius borrowed from the Greek novelistic tradition. Encolpius' adventures can be seen either as centred around certain individuals that he meets (Agamemnon, Quartilla, Trimalchio, Eumolpus, Lichas and Tryphaena, Circe), or as grouped around one location at a time (the school of rhetoric, the brothel, the market-place, the inn, the estate of Trimalchio, the lodgings of the hero, the art gallery, the ship of Lichas, the area outside Croton, Croton). We cannot be absolutely certain that a similar narrative pattern permeated the missing text. Allusions and obscure references found in the surviving novel and in some brief extracts, which cannot now be placed with certainty in particular episodes, allow us to speculate that the missing novel included an oracle urging Encolpius to travel, an incident between Encolpius, Lichas, and Lichas' wife Hedyle, a sexual encounter between Encolpius and Tryphaena, the first meeting between Encolpius and Giton, the robbery (and possibly the murder) of a certain Lycurgus, the acquaintance of Encolpius and Ascyltus, the secret rites of the priestess Quartilla in honour of Priapus, and certain events related to the disappearance of a dirty tunic, which con- tained hidden treasure. The allusions to those incidents are duly pointed out in the endnotes to this translation.

The first scene of the extant text is set at a school of rhetoric in a deliberately unnamed city on the bay of Naples, where Encolpius, accompanied by Ascyltus, is discussing with the teacher Agamemnon the reasons for the decline of Roman education. It

soon becomes clear that Encolpius is neither genuinely interested
in improving the school curriculum nor wishes sincerely to attack
the impractical and unrealistic lessons that were usually delivered
to the students, but is hoping to find a victim who will provide him
and his companions with a free meal, and has spotted his victim in
the person of Agamemnon, who has probably been delivering a
speech at the time of Encolpius' appearance. (In fact, Encolpius'
plan succeeds, since it is the teacher of rhetoric who will lead them
to Trimalchio's dinner-party.)

During the heated conversation between Agamemnon and
Encolpius Ascyltus slips away and, as the hero finds out later on,
returns to their lodgings and attempts to rape Giton. In the
meantime, Encolpius leaves the school of rhetoric, but loses his
way and ends up in a brothel, where he meets Ascyltus, who also
claims to have lost his way and to have been deliberately misled to
that place. When they reach their room, Giton complains in a
superbly melodramatic manner that Ascyltus tried to rape him; this
gives rise to a rhetorical quarrel, the first of three in the extant text,
between Encolpius and Ascyltus. There follows a comic episode in
a market-place, where the heroes try to sell a stolen cloak, but the
person interested in buying it turns out to be not only its legal
owner, but also the possessor of the dirty tunic, which was lost and
which contained treasure.

The priestess Quartilla reappears in the plot. She visits the heroes'
lodgings, sheds false tears, and informs the awestruck Encolpius and
his companions that by witnessing the Priapic rites they have
committed a horrible crime, which has made her catch a severe chill.
The sole remedy for her and the only way to appease Priapus is the
heroes' participation in Priapic rituals, which she herself has already
organised. These are clearly obscene and disagreeable to the hero.

Then Encolpius, Ascyltus, and Giton accept Agamemnon's invitation to dinner at the house of the wealthy freedman Trimalchio,
and have a visually stunning experience at the dining room of this
effeminate, vulgar, arrogant, pretentious, superstitious and morbid
multimillionaire, who is probably Petronius' finest literary creation.
Encolpius' misfortunes, however, do not end when the three lovers
manage to escape from Trimalchio's labyrinthine house: Encolpius
and Ascyltus quarrel over Giton yet again, but this time the
beautiful and unfaithful slave boy decides to opt for Ascyltus, not

Encolpius, as his partner-in-life. The heartbroken hero goes to an art gallery to forget, and there he meets Eumolpus, a lecherous 'manic poetaster' (P. G. Walsh's happy definition), who composes and recites poetry all the time, although his audiences do not appreciate his talents and throw stones at him. Eumolpus will stay with Encolpius and Giton until the end of the surviving novel.

Next there is a melodramatic reconciliation between the suffering hero and his unfaithful young concubine, who manage to get rid of Ascyltus for the rest of the extant text. The following episode takes place on board a ship, which belongs to Lichas and happens to be conveying Tryphaena, both of whom are enemies of Encolpius from the past. Encolpius and Giton are terrified and, with the help of Eumolpus, try to pass unnoticed. Their own tricks betray them, and a mock war breaks out on board the ship, but the heroes avoid punishment when Giton threatens to castrate himself. Reconciliation ensues and an atmosphere of peace, calm, and happiness reigns supreme – but not for long; a storm causes a shipwreck, during which Lichas drowns, Tryphaena manages to escape with the help of her servants, while Encolpius and Giton address each other with brilliantly hackneyed soliloquies filled with conventional pathos and reminiscent of the last words of dying heroines in nineteenth-century operas.

Encolpius, Giton and Eumolpus survive and travel towards Croton, where legacy-hunting dominates. In order to deceive the inhabitants of this decadent town, which (they are told) is famous for its abnormal customs, they devise a theatrical trick: Eumolpus pretends to be a childless millionaire who is about to die, while Encolpius, Giton and the servant Corax pretend to be his slaves. During his stay at Croton Encolpius assumes the Homeric name Polyaenus, and falls in love with a high-class nymphomaniac matron called Circe. His impotence, however, overpowers him, and two ancient witches are called to restore his virility. Both of them fail. Encolpius, however, does regain his sexual power at Croton with the help of Mercury, the patron saint of thieves. What follows is Eumolpus' will, according to which his (fictional) slaves are set free, while his other heirs, the Crotonians, are requested to mutilate Eumolpus and eat his body in public, if they wish to inherit his (imaginary) wealth. The extant text stops at this point.

Is this the ending of the novel? If Encolpius is a caricature of the epic hero Odysseus, and the *Satyricon* a parody of the *Odyssey*, as some have suggested, it may be reasonable to assume that there were originally twenty-four books of Encolpius' adventures. In fact, the majority of the scholars who have dealt with the reconstruction of the final lost part of the novel speak of a pretended death, in which Eumolpus' allegedly dead body is a dummy or someone else's corpse or the flesh of dead animals, while Eumolpus and his trusted servants escape, either with the help of Circe's maid Chrysis, who in the meantime has fallen in love with Encolpius, or after a brawl with the angry Crotonians. But even if that were the case, it would be unwise to expect a conventionally happy conclusion, in which a sexually potent Encolpius would renounce his former life of theft, (possibly) murder, seduction, and homosexual practices, in order to settle down with his former girlfriend Doris, who, as a second Penelope, would have been expecting him faithfully all this time at the place from which Encolpius originally departed. The situation becomes even more speculative and complicated if we consider the possibility that Petronius may not have finished the *Satyricon*, either because he died or because he simply did not want to finish it.

More important, however, than the reconstruction of the ending of the text is establishing Petronius' purpose (if any) in writing this amusing series of immoral adventures, a controversial issue which has plagued Petronian scholarship. Two main theories have recently been put forth to answer this vital question: one supports the notion that the *Satyricon* was no more than a sophisticated and scabrous book, which was composed as a literary joke for Petronius, highly educated close friends. The arguments for this view, forcefully stated by P. G. Walsh, focus on Petronius' character as portrayed by Tacitus, the meaning of the novel's title, the personality of the amoral protagonist Encolpius, the influence of the entertaining but not morally edifying Roman mime, and the dense literary qualities of the *Satyricon*, which do not seem to convey a clear moral message.

The other theory, whose origins date back to the 1940s, interprets this novel as genuine Epicurean propaganda promoting restraint from the pleasures of luxurious food and sex, and freedom from violent passions, the principles of life which the philosopher Epicurus was advocating. It sees Petronius as a great

moralist deliberately depicting a society which is gradually dete-
riorating through luxury and greed, with Trimalchio, his wife and
his guests being the prime examples of this social disease; moreover, in the Neronian age of fear and political chaos the
exaggerated histrionics of the novel's protagonists, Encolpius and
Giton, have been interpreted as their desperate attempts to define
themselves as individuals and to fill the content of their inner
selves, while the learned and refined Petronius is assumed to be
sadly yearning for the glorious literary past, which was, by his
time, an era of sterile declamatory works, irretrievably lost. For
many scholars the question of Petronius' aim remains open, and it
is by no means certain that the discovery of the missing text
would decode the meaning of Encolpius' bawdy adventures.

In fact, at the risk of stating the obvious, it is important to note
that there are two aspects to the protagonist of the *Satyricon*,
Encolpius the actor and Encolpius the narrator, and that neither
should be identified with the author of the text; the former
Encolpius is a young rogue, who leads an adventurous life full of
intensely sexual escapades, whereas the latter Encolpius is a learned
man, whose life is so heavily influenced by the schools of rhetoric
and their practices that, in narrating his past, he cannot help
refashioning his earlier adventures in terms of sublime literature,
especially epic, tragedy, and oratory. This dichotomy, which is not
always clear in the text, as it is often difficult to distinguish
Encolpius the narrator from Petronius the omnipresent author, has
received a great deal of scholarly attention (see, most recently, Gian
Biagio Conte's extremely valuable study), and one example from
the surviving text of the way in which Petronius mocks Encolpius
(in both capacities, as actor and narrator) will suffice to demon-
strate the comedy engendered by such a narrative device. In one of
the episodes, Encolpius 'the actor' has been betrayed by Giton,
who abandons him for the erotic services of Ascyltus. The protagonist's fury, while looking for his lover and his rival, is effectively
presented by Encolpius 'the narrator' as the wrath of the Homeric
warrior Achilles, when his slave girl Briseis was taken from him to
be given to Agamemnon, or as the frenzy of the Virgilian hero
Aeneas, frantically searching for his wife Creusa on the night of
burning Troy.

Thus the uninteresting and banal situation of a homosexual trio has suddenly acquired grandeur and importance, because Encolpius 'the narrator', infatuated with literary myth, has reconstructed an incident of his past as stylised melodrama, which bears the marks of high literature and the lessons taught at the school of rhetoric. It is at this point in the narrative that the deflation of the high tone is achieved: Petronius 'the hidden author' (as Conte cleverly names him) introduces in the plot a passing soldier, who notices that Encolpius is wearing non-military white shoes (the incongruity might be conveyed today by the image of a soldier in pink socks), robs him of his arms, and demolishes the whole melodrama!

It is instructive to observe in the above example that, although this episode loses none of its comic power if the modern reader does not take into account the Homeric context of the scene, it achieves a maximum farcical effect if s/he is aware of the great classical epics. Both here and elsewhere in the text, though, it would be unwise to insist that Petronius had only one literary model in mind, either the Homeric passage or the Virgilian lines or (for that matter) any other similar fictional episode. The unique literary quality of the *Satyricon* lies in the complex combination of its literary components, a combination which justifies J. P. Sullivan's definition of Petronius as a 'literary opportunist'. On the other hand, these epic allusions, like the various poems which are incorporated in the text, and the innumerable other literary echoes, some of which are pointed out in the endnotes, do not serve a merely decorative purpose, but are subtly and carefully integrated in the narrative to heighten Encolpius' pathos. Likewise, the Milesian Tale of the Pergamene Boy, narrated by the old poet Eumolpus, not only provides an opportunity for light relief, but functions also on the level of characterisation, since it portrays Eumolpus as a hypocritical lover of young boys, and foreshadows his future role as Encolpius' rival for the charms of Giton. This multiple function of learned references and the complicated exploitation of formative genres argue against viewing the *Satyricon* as mere pornography, and keep it both refreshingly comic and academically challenging for students and scholars alike.

COSTAS PANAYOTAKIS
University of Glasgow

OTHER MODERN TRANSLATIONS

W. Arrowsmith, *The Satyricon*, New American Library 1960
J. P. Sullivan, *The Satyricon*, Penguin Classics 1986 (rev. ed.)
R. Bracht Branham and Daniel Kinney, *Satyrica*, London 1996
P. G. Walsh, *The Satyricon*, World's Classics 1997

SUGGESTIONS FOR FURTHER READING

N. Holzberg, *The Ancient Novel: an Introduction*, London 1995
G. Schmeling (ed.), *The Novel in the Ancient World*, E. J. Brill 1996
J. P. Sullivan, *The Satyricon of Petronius: A Literary Study*, London 1968
P. G. Walsh, *The Roman Novel*, Cambridge University Press 1970; Bristol Classical Press 1995
N. W. Slater, *Reading Petronius*, Baltimore 1990
C. Panayotakis, *Theatrum Arbitri: Theatrical Elements in the Satyrica of Petronius*, E. J. Brill 1995
G. B. Conte, *The Hidden Author: An Interpretation of Petronius' Satyricon*, Berkeley 1997

Henry Fielding, *Tom Jones*
Henry Fielding, *Joseph Andrews*
F. Scott Fitzgerald, *The Great Gatsby*
James Joyce, *Ulysses*
Henryk Sienkiewicz, *Quo Vadis*
David Wishart, *Nero*

Federico Fellini, *Fellini – Satyricon* (available on video). Note that this extraordinary film is not *Petronius' Satyricon* or simply *Satyricon*, but *Fellini – Satyricon*, that is, Fellini's highly personal interpretation of Petronius' text, not a faithful cinematic rendering of either the plot or of the hilarious tone of this novel. Some film critics regarded this fine film as the late Italian director's masterpiece, while some Petronian scholars found it a boring hotch-potch of Latin literature; Fellini himself defined it as 'a science-fiction view of ancient Rome'.

NOTE ON THE TRANSLATION

This translation was originally commissioned by John Lehmann for his publishing house, and I followed the text edited by F. Bücheler (Berlin, 1871) and the *Cena Trimalchionis* of W. Heraeus (1909), with considerable reference to the textual edition of Alfred Ernout (Paris, 1950). The present revision has been further aided by M. S. Smith's critical edition of the *Cena Trimalchionis* (1975).

P. D.

LIST OF CHARACTERS

The scene is Southern Italy, in a Campanian town somewhere near Naples; later, aboard the ship that will be wrecked in the Bay of Tarentum, and lastly in the harbour-city of Croton, in the toe of Italy. The narrator throughout is Encolpius, an irresponsible, vagabond student who is discovered denouncing modern rhetoric in favour of the ancient style. The other principal characters are:

Agamemnon, a teacher of rhetoric
Ascyltus, Encolpius' friend and accomplice
Giton, a boy of sixteen attached to Encolpius
Quartilla, a local devotee of Priapus; *Psyche*, her maid; *Pannychis*, a girl of seven, with Quartilla
Trimalchio, a millionaire freedman; *Menelaus*, his aide; *Fortunata*, his wife
Dama, *Seleucas*, *Phileros*, *Ganymede* and *Echion*, freedmen
Niceros, *Plocamus*, freedmen, friends of Trimalchio
Daedalus, Trimalchio's cook
Croesus, Trimalchio's favourite boy
Habinnas, a freedman and stonemason; *Scintilla*, his wife; *Massa*, his slave
Eumolpus, an old reprobate poet
Marcus Mannicius, a landlord
Bargates, the manager of a lodging-house
Lichas, a ship's owner, captain and businessman
Tryphaena, a woman of pleasure and Lichas' associate

Hesus, a passenger aboard ship
Chrysis, maid to Circe
Circe, Encolpius' would-be mistress
Proselenus, *Oenothea*, old women

Two animals are named: *Scylax*, Trimalchio's mastiff, and *Margarita*, Croesus' bitch.

SATYRICON

II

The adventures at the school of rhetoric and the brothel[1]

'But are they not the same Furies that torment our public speakers?[2] Those who cry, "These wounds I got defending the people's liberty! This eye was lost for you! Give me a guide, lead me to my children, for my mangled limbs will not support me!"? Even this might be tolerated if it put beginners on the high road to eloquence. But with such turgid themes and hollow, rattling phrases, all it comes down to is this: once at the bar, they imagine themselves set down in another world. And so I think that what makes learners in the schools masters of idiocy is that they neither see nor hear anything of the common run of life; but it must be pirates stranded on the beach in chains, tyrants ordering sons to sever paternal heads, or oracular answers in time of plague which mean the immolation of three virgins at least – nothing but honey-ball conceits, everything, word and deed, as it were powdered with poppy and sesame.

Brought up on this diet, what taste can they have acquired? Don't those who live in kitchens always smell of the pot? You, if you don't mind my saying so, were the first to stifle eloquence. Reducing it to trivial, hollow sounds, to a mockery, you have succeeded in depriving oratory of its sinews and life-blood. The young were far from shackled to these stock declamations when Sophocles and Euripides[3] forged the language they wanted to use. Your hole-and-corner professor had not yet destroyed genius when Pindar and the nine lyric poets[4] flinched from Homer's rhythms. And not to quote mere poets in support, I can see beyond any doubt that neither Plato nor Demosthenes[5] went in for this kind of exercise. Great and, if I may say so, deferential speech is neither raddled nor bloated, but rises in its own natural beauty. Only recently this monstrous, wind-filled blabbering[6] settled out of Asia on Athens like the influence of some noxious planet and blasted the aspiring talents of our youth. Once the rules were broken, eloquence ceased and fell silent. In fine, after this, who reached such renown as Thucydides or Hyperides?[7] Even poetry lost its brilliance and healthy colour, and everything nourished on the same food failed to attain white-headed old age. Painting as well came to just such a bad end after the Egyptians impudently devised short cuts to that great art.'

3   Agamemnon was unable to put up with hearing me declaim in the portico for longer than he himself had sweated it out in school. 'Young man,' he said, 'because you speak in defiance of public taste and, a very rare thing, you love good sense, I won't keep the secrets of our art from you. Of course the masters are not to blame for these exercises, since they must by necessity rave with their idiots. Unless they teach what is acceptable to the young, then "they will be left alone in the schools," as Cicero says. Just as toadies trying to scrounge a supper from the rich only consider things most likely to please the company, for they never get what they are after unless they set traps for the ears, so with your teacher of rhetoric; unless he baits his hook like a fisherman with what he knows the fry will snap at, he will idle on a rock with no hope of a catch.

4   'What is the answer? Parents are the ones to be blamed, not wanting their children to progress under any discipline. Like everyone else, the first thing they do is dedicate their young hopefuls to ambition. Then, to lend wings to their wishes, they hustle these green schoolboys to the courts, and would drape rhetoric – and they admit there is nothing greater – round children who are still babes in arms. If only they allowed them to study step by step, so that studious youths were absorbed in grave readings, their minds imbued with wise maxims, their pens unsparing in correction, so that they listened patiently to the models they had a mind to imitate, and if only parents were convinced that anything taking a child's fancy is of no consequence, then the great oratory that we knew would once more assume its majesty and significance. Nowadays children play at their schools, our young men are mocked in the courts, and worse than either of these things, in old age they will not admit to the erroneous learning of their youth. But don't think I am jibing at a modest impromptu in the style of Lucilius;[8] here is a poem of my own to express what I feel.'

If any would master a rigorous art, and set his mind on the sublime, let him first improve his character by a strict rule of austerity. He shall not respect the insolent palace's high façade, nor crawl for suppers like a discredited client, nor be damned and dowse his spiritual fire with wine, nor shall he sit in the claque of a playhouse crying up the actors. But whether armed Athens' fortress smiles on him, or the land where the Spartan farmer lives, or the Sirens,[9] let him give his first years to poetry, and fill his carefree heart at Homer's well; then, sated with the Socratic school, shake off his leading-strings, and flourish free the weapons of great Demosthenes. Let Roman society flock about him and, Greekish accents gone, change his taste and imbue his soul. Out of court, let his pen at times run free, to sing varied Fortune in her skittish course, then feasts, and wars told in heroic song, and high-sounding words such as fell from intrepid Cicero. To which good end gird up your mind, and from your heart, filled at these ample streams, pour words the Muses love.'

I was listening so attentively that I did not notice Ascyltus had given me the slip . . .

And then as I paced the garden in the heat of conversation, a great crowd of students appeared in the portico, apparently having left somebody whose extempore speech had followed Agamemnon's set topic. While the young men ridiculed his phrases and slandered his whole concept of style, I seized the chance of making off, and sped after Ascyltus. But I could not remember the way very well, I did not know where our lodgings were. So whichever way I turned, I kept coming back to the same place. I was tired out with running, and all of a sweat. I accosted an old woman who was selling country vegetables.

'Tell me, mother,' I said, 'do you happen to know where I live?'

Delighted by this rather ingenuous quip, she said, 'Why not?' and got up and began to lead the way. I took her for a soothsayer and . . .

We soon reached a place off the beaten track, and the obliging old woman threw back a patched curtain and said, 'This is where you ought to live.'

I was denying that I knew the house, and then I saw some men furtively picking their way among price-labels and naked prostitutes. Too late, too late indeed, I realised that I had been diverted into a bawdy-house. I swore at the sly old hag, covered my head, and ran through the brothel to the other side. There, right on the doorstep, as tired as I and as near dead, was Ascyltus. You would have thought the same old woman had brought him there. I greeted him with a laugh and asked him what he was doing in this frightful place. He mopped his sweating brow.

8 'If you only knew,' he said, 'what has happened to me.'

'What?' I asked. He was nearly fainting.

'I was wandering about all over the town,' he said, 'and couldn't find the place where I left our lodgings, when a respectable-looking man came up and very kindly offered to show me the way. He led me round some dark, tortuous lanes and brought me out here, then his money was in his hand and he began to propose debauchery. The bawd had already taken a coin for the room, and now the man seized me, and if I hadn't been stronger than he was, I would have been in for it.'

*   *   *

Everybody, everywhere, seemed to be drunk on aphrodisiacs.

*   *   *

Combining our forces, we repulsed the troublemaker.[10]

*   *   *

9 As through a mist I saw Giton standing on a street-corner, and I hastened towards him.

I asked my brother[11] whether he had got anything ready for us to eat, and the boy sat on the bed and wiped away his welling tears with his thumb. The state he was in alarmed me, and I asked him what had happened. He was hesitant, loath to speak, but after some anger began to show in my entreaties, he said, 'It's that brother of yours, your fellow-adventurer, who came running into our rooms not long ago and started to take me by force. When I shouted, he drew his sword. "If you're Lucretia," he said, "you've met your Tarquin."'[12]

I shook my fist in Ascyltus' face when I heard this. 'What do you say to this,' I cried, 'you stinking-breathed queen?'

Ascyltus feigned indignation, then put up his fists and roared the louder, 'Shut up, you filthy cut-throat![13] You disgraced reject from the ring! Shut up, you night-time slasher! In your prime you couldn't have it out with a clean woman. I was the same kind of brother to you in the garden as the boy is in your lodgings.'

'You sneaked off from our tutor's lecture,' I said.   10

'You idiot, what did you expect me to do? I was dying of hunger. Stay and listen to his theories, all glittering fragments and the meaning of dreams? Damned if you're not far worse than me, praising a poet to get asked out to supper.'

And our sordid mud-slinging turned to laughter, and we proceeded more calmly to other things.

*   *   *

But his mischief rankled in my mind. 'Ascyltus,' I said, 'I can see we shall never agree. We will split our baggage and try to keep poverty at bay each on his own. You're educated, so am I. I won't stand in your way, I'll take up some other line, otherwise we shall clash over a hundred things every day and be the talk of the town.'

Ascyltus did not object. 'As scholars,' he said, 'we are due for a dinner tonight, so we shall not waste the evening. Tomorrow, as you so wish, I shall look for new rooms and another companion.'

'It's a bore delaying one's pleasure,' I remarked.

*   *   *

Passion caused this rash separation, for I had long wanted to rid myself of this importunate watchdog and resume my old ways with Giton.

*   *   *

I went sight-seeing all over the town, then returned to my little   11
room. I exchanged kisses without inhibition, entered the closest embrace, and fulfilled my desires with a happiness to be envied. We had still not finished when Ascyltus crept up to the door, loudly sprang back the bolt and came in, with me still at play with my brother. His laughter and applause filled the room.

He pulled off the cloak that covered me and cried, 'What are you doing, my most virtuous brother? What? Two of you in the same tent?'

And not content with mere words, he took the strap from his bag and began to thrash me in no perfunctory manner, putting in some caustic remarks: 'So this is share and share alike with your brother! Don't do it!'

2

The adventure of the stolen tunic and
Quartilla's staged orgy

Dusk was falling when we reached the market. We saw no end of 12
things for sale, not of any great value, though the half-dark did
much to veil their dubious worth. As we had brought our stolen
cloak[1] with us, we seized an excellent opportunity of flourishing
one end of it in a corner of the market, hoping to tempt a buyer by
the garment's brilliant colour. We did not wait long. A rustic,
whose face was familiar, came up with a chit of a woman and began
to run his eye over the cloak attentively. Ascyltus in turn contem-
plated the back of our country customer, and drew in his breath
sharply with amazement. I myself could not look at the fellow
without some agitation, for I seemed to recognise the man who
found our shirt in the waste land. In fact it was he. But Ascyltus
dared not believe his own eyes, and to avoid leaving it to chance he
first edged up like a purchaser, then pulled the shirt off his
shoulders and fingered it thoroughly.

The vagaries of fortune! By a miracle, the boor had never laid his 13
prying hand on the seams, and rather disdainfully had it for sale as
a beggar's cast-off. When Ascyltus saw that our savings were safe
and that the seller was a contemptible specimen, he took me a little
to one side of the crowd.

'Would you believe, my dear,' he said, 'the treasure I complained of losing has turned up? This is our old shirt, and still full of
gold by the looks of it. What should we do? What steps can we take
to claim what's ours?'

I was overjoyed, not only because I saw something to be gained,
but because fate had cleared me of the worst suspicions.[2] I was
against any indirect action. We should contend in the open, by

civil rights, and if they refused to return to its owner property that did not belong to them, we would have recourse to disposal by the courts.

14   Ascyltus, on the other hand, was afraid of the law. 'Who knows us here?' he said. 'Who will believe a word we say? I would prefer to buy it, although we can see it is ours. Better to spend a little money getting back our wealth than embark on a legal dispute.

> What use are laws where money alone is king,
> And poverty never can carry the day?
> Those who anatomise the age with the Cynic's scrip[3]
> At times are known to sell the truth for cash.
> So justice is a general commodity,
> And the knight who sits on your case
> Proves this or that by what he's paid.'

But apart from a mite with which we intended to buy chickpeas and lupins, we had nothing in hand. So to stop our prize vanishing in the meantime, we decided to knock down our cloak even more cheaply. A greater return would compensate for this negligible loss. But just as we were spreading out our goods, a woman in a veil who stood next to the rustic first closely examined the marks on the cloak, then snatched it with both hands and shouted at the top of her voice, 'Thieves!'

We were disconcerted, but rather than do nothing, we heaved at the tattered, dirty shirt and protested with no less venom that they had some spoil belonging to us. But it was in no way an even match. The dealers who flocked to the brawl laughed at our claim, as they well might, seeing one side demand a most valuable cloak, and the other a bundle of rags not even good enough for patchwork!

15   Then Ascyltus managed to stop their laughter, and when there was silence, he said, 'We can all see that everyone loves what is his own; well, if they will give us back our shirt, they shall have their cloak.'

The man and his woman agreed to the exchange, but some officers of the law, or more probably prowlers by night who wanted their share out of the cloak, insisted that we left both garments in their hands and let the judge examine our complaint the next day. For it seemed that not only were these objects in dispute, but there was also a very different matter, that is to say, each party lay under suspicion of larceny. The idea of trustees found favour, and one of the dealers, a bald man with a lumpy forehead who had worked for the law on and off, had already got hold of the cloak and declared he would produce it the next day. But it was clear that these thieves only intended to hush up the matter once the cloak was in their hands, keeping us from our appointment for fear of a criminal charge.

This was clearly our wish too; and by chance the wishes of either side were gratified. Outraged because we asked for his rags to be exposed to view, the countryman flung the shirt in Ascyltus' face, and having put paid to our grievances, he told us to deposit the cloak that had started the whole argument.

We had got back our savings, or so we thought, and we ran full tilt to our lodgings. Behind closed doors we fell to laughing at the sharp practice of the dealers and of our accusers too, whose excessive smartness had returned our money to us.

> What I want, I would like at my leisure,
> A ready-made win is never a pleasure.[4]

*   *   *

We had scarcely swallowed the supper Giton had been good 16 enough to get ready for us when the door shook under an authoritative knock. We turned pale and asked who it was.

'Open up and find out,' said a voice. While we were still speaking, the bolt gave way on its own and fell off, the door burst open and let our visitor in. It was a woman in a veil, the same who had been with the rustic not so long ago.

'Did you think you'd put one over on me?' she asked. 'I am Quartilla's maid, whose rite you interrupted by the grotto.[5] She has come to your place in person, and would like to speak to you. Don't be alarmed. She will neither blame you nor punish you for your mistake. On the contrary, she is wondering what god has conferred such agreeable young men on her neighbourhood!'

We sat dumb, and ventured no agreement one way or the other. 17 Then Quartilla herself came in with a girl by her side and, sitting on my bed, wept for some time. No word left our lips as we still waited in bewilderment for the end of these tears, an ostentatious show of grief. When the artificial shower had run dry she uncovered her proud head and wrung her hands together until the joints cracked.

'What devilry is this?' she cried. 'Where did you learn to do even better than the brigands of fiction? I am indeed very sorry for you. No one looks on forbidden things without being punished. Besides, there are so many deities in these parts that a god is sooner encountered than a man. But don't think I come here for revenge. Your youth affects me more than your wronging me, and I have always believed that ignorance led you into a crime that can never be propitiated. That very night I was seized with such dreadful cold shivers I was afraid I had the tertian ague. I begged for a cure in my sleep, and was told to track you down and assuage my feverish attacks by a cunning means that would be revealed to me. But I am not that concerned with the remedy. A greater grief runs wild in my heart and draws me down to inescapable death. For I fear the indiscretion of your years will make you divulge what you saw at the shrine of Priapus, and you will come out in public with the counsels of the gods. So at your very knees I raise my hands to you, I beg and pray you will not make sport or a butt of our nocturnal cult, nor decry age-old mysteries known to barely a thousand mortals.'

18   A new flood of tears followed this appeal and, convulsed with heavy sobs, she buried her face and bosom on my bed. Pity and fear combined to upset me. I tried to give her heart and told her not to worry about either matter, for none of us would betray her sacred rites, and if a god had prescribed her some extraordinary remedy for her tertian ague, we would certainly back up divine providence, and risk our lives to do so. At this promise the woman cheered up, kissed me close and full, and as her tears turned to laughter she played with the long hair that fell about my ears.

'I'll make my peace,' she said, 'and withdraw the charge I laid against you. But if you had not agreed to let me have the cure I want, tomorrow would have seen a whole mob ready to avenge my wrong and restore my honour.

> Disdain is shameful, to lay down the law superb;
> I love to go my own way, as indeed I can.
> Even the philosopher argues when scorned;
> But the man who pardons is your true victor.'

*   *   *

Then with a clap of her hands she suddenly gave vent to such loud laughter that we were frightened by it. And as for the maid who came in ahead, she did the same, and so did the little girl who came in with her. The whole place rang with melodramatic laughter. 19 We saw no reason for this unexpected change of face, and we first gazed at each other and then at the women.

*   *   *

'What is more, I forbade any living soul to enter this lodging-house today, so that I could receive the remedy for my tertian ague from you without interruption.'

When Quartilla said this, Ascyltus was paralysed for a moment, and I turned colder than a winter in Gaul, unable to utter a word. But our combined strength was such that I foresaw no trouble. They were three women of no size or strength, if they had a mind to attack us; especially us, who were superior by sex, if nothing else. Besides, we were certainly in fighting trim, and more than that, I had already matched off the pairs, and if it came to a show-down, I would settle for Quartilla, Ascyltus for the maid, and Giton for the girl.

*   *   *

But at this point our self-possession all gave way, we were bewildered, and the shadow of certain death began to fall across our unhappy eyes.[6]

*   *   *

'Please, madam,' I said, 'if you have something more unpleasant in 20 store for us, get it over quickly. Our crime is not so great that we ought to die by torture.'

*   *   *

The maid, whose name was Psyche, carefully spread a blanket on the floor.

*   *   *

She tried to excite me. I was as cold as if I had died a thousand deaths.

*   *   *

Ascyltus had covered his head with his cloak. He had learnt that it is dangerous to pry into other people's secrets.

*   *   *

The maid took two strips from a fold of her dress and bound our feet with one and our hands with the other.

*   *   *

Ascyltus saw that the conversation flagged. 'What?' he said. 'Don't I get a drink?'

The maid was betrayed by my laughter. She clapped her hands: 'But I served you, young man. Have you drunk all the potion yourself?'

'No, really,' said Quartilla, 'has Encolpius swallowed the whole aphrodisiac?'

*   *   *

A ripple of pleasant laughter shook her sides.

*   *   *

In the end even Giton had to laugh, especially when the girl threw her arms round his neck and gave him countless kisses, at which he did not demur.

*   *   *

21 We wanted to cry out in our plight, but there was no one there to help us, and every time I tried to summon worthy citizens to the rescue, Psyche pricked at my cheeks with a hair-pin, and the girl kept Ascyltus at bay with a sponge sopping with aphrodisiac.

*   *   *

To crown it all, a catamite arrived in hairy clothes of myrtle-green tucked to the waist. First he flattened us with his writhing buttocks. Then he slobbered rank kisses over us, until Quartilla, with a whalebone wand in her hand and her dress above her knees, ordered us wretches to be given quarter.

*   *   *

We both swore a most solemn oath that we would carry the horrid secret to our graves.

*   *   *

A crowd of wrestling-school professionals came in, rubbed us down with pure oil, and set us on our feet once more. Somehow our weariness vanished. We put our dinner-clothes on again, and were shown into the next room, where three couches were laid out, and the whole magnificent array of a banquet. We were asked to take our places, and began with some wonderful *entrées*, besides being plied with Falernian wine.[7] We followed a number of courses through and were sinking to sleep, when Quartilla exclaimed, 'Now then! The idea of going to sleep, when you know the whole night is dedicated in honour of Priapus!'

*   *   *

Heavy with so many troubles, Ascyltus was drowsing off when the   22
maid he had so rudely repulsed smeared his face all over with soot and painted his lips and neck, without his feeling a thing. I too, burdened and weary, had taken a bare foretaste of sleep, and all the indoor servants and the outdoor ones were doing the same. Some lay about here and there at the feet of guests, some were hugging the walls, and some stayed in the doorways with their heads on each other's shoulders. The lamps were low in oil and spread a thin and dying light. Just then, two Syrians came in to pilfer from the dining-room, and quarrelling greedily over so much silverware, pulled a jar apart and broke it. Over went the table with all its plate. A cup flew off and fell from a height on a maid lolling on one of the couches, and nearly split her head open. Her scream at this blow betrayed the rascals and woke some of the drunkards. The thieving Syrians realised they had been detected, dropped on a couch together with such precision that it might have been rehearsed, and began to snore like veteran sleepers.

By now the butler was up. He poured oil into the failing lamps. The slaves rubbed their eyes for a moment or two and went back to their duties. Then a cymbal-player came in, roused everybody with her crashing brass, and the evening began again. Quartilla   23
called us to drinking once more, and the girl with the cymbals enlivened our revels.

*   *   *

In came an effeminate creature, of all beings the most washed-out specimen, and evidently very much at home in this place. He clapped his limp hands together and spouted a song something like this:

> Quick, quick now, come now, luscious boys,
> Stretch a leg, heat the pace, twirl on the sole,
> Soft thighs, brisk buttocks, and impudent hands,
> Oh, tender, oh, tough, oh, Delos' geldings!

When he finished his verses he gave me a most filthy, spittle-covered kiss. Then he planted himself on my bed, and unwilling though I was, used all his strength in undressing me. He laboured hard and long upon me, and to no effect. His sweating brow poured with little streams of paint, and there was so much chalk-white in the wrinkles of his cheeks you would have thought them walls washed out by a rainstorm.

24   I could hold back my tears no longer, and reduced to utter misery, 'Please, madam,' I said, 'didn't you say I was to be given a sleeper's potion?'

She clapped her hands lightly and said, 'The clever young man! Fount of native wit! Don't you know that our sleeper means just that?'[8]

Then, so my fellow should be no better off than myself, I said, 'Upon your honour, is Ascyltus to be the only one idle in the whole room?'

'Very well,' said Quartilla, 'let's give Ascyltus one.'

On this order, the man changed mounts, and once with my companion, ground him with buttocks and kisses. Giton stood in the middle and split his sides with laughter. Whereupon Quartilla noticed him and enquired with great interest whose boy he was. I said he was mine.

'Why hasn't he kissed me then?' she asked. She called him over and gave him a kiss.

Then she slid her hand beneath his dress and fondled an inexperienced part: 'This,' she said, 'shall serve gallantly as the first course of our pleasures tomorrow; today, having feasted so well, I am exacting no pittance.'

25   At this point Psyche came laughing up to her and whispered something in her ear.

'Yes, indeed,' said Quartilla, 'you were right to remind me. Why not? Wouldn't this be a splendid opportunity of winning our dear Pannychis' maidenhead?'

An attractive girl was brought in who did not appear to be more than seven years old, and the very one who had come to our lodgings with Quartilla. Everybody applauded and clamoured for the wedding ceremony. I was thunderstruck, and protested that neither could Giton, the most bashful of all boys, stand up to this wantonness, nor was the girl of an age to submit to the marital act.

'What,' said Quartilla, 'is she younger than I was when I lost my virginity? May Juno revile me if I remember ever having been a virgin! For as a child I went to it with those of my own age, and as the years passed I applied myself to bigger boys, and so came to the age where I am. I think this gave rise to a proverb they have: who has carried the calf, can bear the bull.'

I got up for the wedding, afraid some greater ill might happen to 26 my brother on his own.

Psyche had already covered the girl's brow with a veil. Our 'sleeping potion' carried the torch in front, behind him came a long rout of drunken, clapping women, who had prepared the bridal chamber with lewd draperies. Aroused by this ludicrous parody, Quartilla next sprang up herself, seized Giton and dragged him into the bedroom. Truth to tell, the puppy was not unwilling, and the girl herself, by no means cheerless, did not blench at the mention of marriage. When they were alone behind closed doors, we sat down on the threshold of the bridal chamber. Well to the fore, Quartilla put her inquisitive eye to a crack made expressly for the purpose of cheating and watched the children at play with indecent persistence. Her caressing hand drew me near to share this sight, our faces brushed together in this position, and whenever she took her eyes away she would pass her lips near mine, now and then to crush a sly kiss upon me.

*   *   *

We jumped into bed and spent the rest of the night without fear.

3

Trimalchio's dinner party

It was now the third day.[1] A free-for-all banquet was in the wind. But after so many harrowing blows, escape was more tempting than rest. As we considered in our dejection how to avoid the storm to come, one of Agamemnon's servants broke in upon our wavering mood.

'What,' he said, 'you don't know where it's taking place? At Trimalchio's,[2] the most fashionable of men, and he has a clock in his dining-room and has hired a trumpeter,[3] just to know from time to time how much of his life he has lost.'

We forgot our troubles and dressed with some care, making Giton, who had been a most willing slave till now, follow us to the baths.

But in the meantime, without undressing, we began to saunter . . . or rather we trifled and mixed with different groups, when suddenly we saw a bald old man in a red shirt[4] playing ball with some long-haired boys.[5] Yet our eyes were drawn not to them, although they were worth it, but to their master, a man in slippers who was occupied with some green balls. He never picked one of them up once it touched the ground; a slave had a bag full and supplied the players. We noticed other novelties. Two eunuchs stood in the field at opposite points; one held a silver chamber-pot, and the other counted the balls, not those that were flung from hand to hand as the game progressed, but those that fell to the ground. As we stood admiring these luxuries, Menelaus[6] ran up to say, 'This is the man whose table you'll be gracing. What you are watching is a prelude to the dinner.'

Menelaus had not finished speaking when Trimalchio snapped his fingers, and the eunuch reached him the chamber-pot while he was still playing. He emptied his bladder, asked for water for

27

his hands, dipped his fingertips in it and wiped them on a boy's
head.

28   It would be tedious to go into every detail. We went to the
baths, and once we were heated in the sweating-room, passed
through to the cold showers. Drenched in perfume, Trimalchio
was rubbed down, not with cloths, but with towels of the softest
wool. Three masseurs were swigging Falernian[7] under his very eyes
and spilling most of it in a quarrel.

'They're drinking my health with my own wine,' said
Trimalchio.

Then they rolled him up in a scarlet housecoat and put him on a
litter. Four runners decked with medallions went in front, with a
go-cart that bore his pet, a wizened, blear-eyed boy[8] more hideous
than his own master. As he set off, a musician with tiny flutes got
close to his headrest and piped the whole way as if he whispered
some secret in his ear. We followed full of wonder, and arrived at
the door with Agamemnon. A notice was stuck on the upright. It
read: *Any slave going outdoors without the master's permission gets one
hundred stripes*. At the entrance was a porter in leek-green livery
with a cherry-red belt, shelling peas into a silver dish. A golden
cage hung over the door, and from it a gaudy magpie hailed all
newcomers.

29   But while struck with wonder at everything, I very nearly fell
backwards and cracked my shins, for not far from the porter's lodge
was a huge dog on a chain painted on the wall, and in capital letters
above: BEWARE OF THE DOG. My friends laughed at me. When I
came to my senses I surveyed the whole wall. It was a mural of a
slave-market, and each slave had a label round his neck.
Trimalchio was there, long-haired, with Mercury's staff in his
hand, entering Rome led by Minerva.[9] Next, how he learned to
keep accounts, and how he eventually became a steward, had all
been carefully depicted with suitable inscriptions by the painstaking artist. Towards the end of the colonnade Mercury was heaving
him into a lofty judgement seat, holding him under the chin. Right
by his side was Fortune with a flowing horn of plenty, and the
three Fates winding out their golden thread. In this place I also
noticed a trainer exercising a troop of couriers. In a corner I saw a
large cupboard in which household gods of silver had been placed
on a shrine; there was a marble statue of Venus, and a gold box of

no mean size in which they said was preserved the beard of the great man himself.[10]

I asked the keeper what pictures they had in the centre of the gallery.

'The Iliad and the Odyssey,' he replied, 'and a show by Laenas' gladiators.'[11]

We could spare no time to consider more . . . We now came to 30 the dining-room, where at the entrance the manager was receiving accounts. But what especially astonished me were bundles of rods with axe-heads protruding, fastened to the doorposts, the end of them finished like the bronze prow of a ship, on which was inscribed: *Cinnamus the Treasurer, to Gaius Pompeius Trimalchio, Priest of Augustus' College.*[12] A twin lamp with the same words on it hung from the arch, and there were two panels on each of the doorposts. One of them, if I remember rightly, had this notice: *On the 30th and 31st December our master Gaius will be dining out.* On the other the phases of the moon and images of the seven stars were painted. Days propitious or unfavourable were noted by different studs.

Full of these delights we started to enter the dining-room, when one of the boys shouted 'Right foot!' This was his job. For a moment we were startled. One of us might break a rule in crossing the threshold. We had scarcely advanced our right feet by a concerted effort when a slave, stripped for flogging, threw himself down before us and begged us to rescue him from punishment. Not that the offence endangering him seemed considerable. He had let the treasurer's clothes be stolen from the baths, and they were worth about ten sesterces. So we withdrew our right feet and pleaded with the treasurer to call off the punishment. He was counting out gold in the hall, and raised his head haughtily: 'It's not so much the loss that irks me, it's the negligence of this ne'er-do-well. He lost my dress-clothes, a birthday present from a particular client of mine. They were real Tyrian purple[13] too, but put through the wash once already. I have nothing more to say. I leave him to you.'

We were much obliged by this favour, and entered the dining- 31 room. The same slave we interceded for ran up to us, and to our astonishment forced a hail of kisses on us, with thanks for our goodwill.

'In short,' he said, 'you shall soon know who you have been of service to. The butler's gratitude is bestowed through his master's wine.'

We finally took our places on the couch. Alexandrian slaves poured snow-water on our hands, while others followed to attend to our feet and pared our toenails with immense dexterity. Even in that exacting duty they did not keep silent, but sang all the time. I wanted to find out if the lot of them could sing, so I ordered a drink, and a boy promptly entertained me with a grating song into the bargain. Whoever was asked for anything did the same. You would have thought it a low cabaret instead of the dining-room of a respectable citizen.

Then an extremely grand first course was served, as all the company was now seated except Trimalchio, for whom the first place at table was still reserved according to a new fashion. For the *hors d'oeuvre* there was a large dish with the figure of an ass on it, in Corinthian bronze, and loaded with twin panniers containing olives, green on one side and black on the other. The ass was sheltered by two flat plates engraved round the rims with Trimalchio's name and their weight in silver. Then little bridges, soldered together, held dormice conserved in honey and sprinkled with poppy-seed. There were piping-hot sausages over a silver grid, with damsons and the seeds of pomegranates below.

32   We were up to our elbows in this magnificence when Trimalchio himself was brought in[14] to the sound of music, supported by diminutive cushions. Some imprudent laughter escaped, for his shaven head only just peeped out of a scarlet cloak, and over the thick garment about his neck he had fastened a napkin with a nobleman's purple stripe and tasselled fringes all round. On the little finger of his left hand he wore a huge gilded ring, and on the end of the next finger a smaller one that seemed to me to be gold through and through, but was entirely composed of star-like points of steel. He wanted to exhibit further riches, and he bared his right arm to reveal a gold armlet and a circle of ivory clasped by a lustrous flat piece of metal.

33   Then, after going over his teeth with a silver toothpick, he said, 'My friends, I would rather not have come to table so soon, but my absence might have delayed you longer, so I put aside all private indulgence. But allow me to finish my game.'

A boy followed him with a board of terebinth wood and crystal checkers. I noticed an exquisite refinement: instead of white and black pieces he had gold and silver coins. In the meantime, while he played his game and exhausted his stock of smut, and while we were still busy with the *hors d'oeuvre*, they served a contrivance which held a basket, and in this was a wooden hen with her wings folded about her as they are when a bird is sitting. Instantly two slaves approached to a burst of music, began to rummage in the straw, and handed out peahens' eggs to the guests. Trimalchio let his gaze fall on this scene.

'Friends,' he explained, 'I ordered the peahens' eggs to be placed under the hen. And, stap me, I'm afraid they might be hatching already, but we'll try and see if they're still good enough to swallow.'

We took our spoons, weighing half a pound each, and broke into the eggs, which were moulded of rich paste. I must say I nearly threw my portion back, for it seemed to have a chick in it. Then I heard a seasoned diner-out saying, 'I don't know, there ought to be something good inside,' and persevered among the shells until, embedded in yolks of egg spiced with pepper, I found a fat fig-pecker.

His game was over, and Trimalchio called for all the same dishes 34 himself, loudly permitting us to take a second glass of mead if we wanted. Suddenly there was a signal from the musicians, and the first course was whisked away in concert by a group of singing servants. What was more, a dessert-dish happened to fall in the hustle. A boy picked it up. Trimalchio, who saw it, ordered him to be cuffed on the ear and made him throw it down again. Then a servant in charge of furniture followed with a broom and swept the silver dish away with the other refuse. After that, two shaggy Ethiopians, like those who strew sand in the amphitheatre, entered with miniature wineskins and poured wine on our hands, for no one had water to offer.

Our host was being complimented on his discriminating taste.

'Mars loves what's right and fair,' he said. 'So I ordered a separate table for each guest. That way these nauseating slaves won't make us so hot with their coming and going.'

There and then they fetched glass bottles, carefully sealed, and round the necks were fastened labels with this legend: *Falernian.*[15] *Bottled under Opimius. A Hundred Years Old.*

While we scanned the labels, Trimalchio clapped his hands and cried, 'How sad that wine keeps longer than a weakling man! So down the hatch with it! Wine is life. This is the real Opimian! I produced something much less good yesterday when a smarter set was dining.'

We drank up and admired the fastidious elegance of everything. Then a slave produced a silver skeleton,[16] so contrived that its limbs and backbone were pliant and permitted movement in any direction. When he had cast it down on the table a few times so that its flexibility had created a number of postures, Trimalchio commented:

> 'Ah, we wretches, insignificant man adds up to nothing:
> We'll all be like this when we're dead and gone.
> Live then, while yet we may live well.'

35   Our applause was followed by a dish hardly as ample as we had expected. But its strangeness drew every eye upon it. It was a round plate with the twelve signs of the Zodiac[17] spaced about the edge, and on each the chef had put a morsel of food suited by nature to its symbol. Over the Ram, ram's head chickpeas; over the Bull, a bit of sirloin; on the Twins, pairs of kidneys and testicles; a crown on the Crab; on the Lion, an African fig; on the Virgin, the womb of a barren sow; on the Balance, a pair of scales with a tart on one side and a honey-cake on the other; over the Scorpion, a small saltwater fish; a hare on the Archer; a langouste over the Goat; a goose on the Water-carrier; and two mullets over the Fishes. In the centre was a fresh-cut sod of turf bearing a honey-comb.

An Egyptian boy took round bread on a silver hotplate . . . even he, in a repulsive voice, ground out a farcical chorus from *The Laserwort Seller*.[18] We confronted this base fare with long faces, and Trimalchio said, 'I suggest we dine now. That is the custom at table.'

36   As he spoke, four servants pranced in rhythmically with the music, and removed the top half of the dish. Below we saw fat spayed hens and sows' udders. And in the middle was a hare trussed up with wings to look like Pegasus. We also noticed at the corners of the dish four figures of Marsyas[19] spouting a peppery garum from their skins over some fish, which swam about in it as in conflicting

tidal currents. We all joined in the applause prompted by the
servants and cheerfully fell upon these delicacies. Trimalchio was
no less elated by this ingenuity, and cried 'Carver!'

Up came the carver at once, and in so many gestures cut the meat
about to the strains of music; you would have thought he was
fighting at the games from a chariot to the sound of the water-
organ. In a low voice Trimalchio was still insisting, 'Carve 'er,
carver!'[20]

Suspecting that this continual repetition was some stroke of wit,
I hazarded a question about it to the man lounging next above me.
He had seen many other such entertainments.

'You see that fellow carving the meat?' he said. 'His name is
Carver. So as often as Trimalchio says "Carve 'er, carver," that
word does duty for both call and order.'

I was unable to swallow anything more, and turned to him to 37
learn as much as I could. I had him start his tittle-tattle from the
beginning by asking who the woman was dashing up and down.

'Trimalchio's wife,' he said. 'She is called Fortunata, and measures
her money by the cartload. And yesterday? What was she yesterday?
Forgive me for saying so, but you wouldn't even have taken bread
out of her hand. Now, and nobody knows how or why, she's in very
heaven, Trimalchio's be-all and end-all. In a word, if she said it was
midnight at high noon, he would believe her. He himself doesn't
know what is his, he's so very rich; but this lynx has eyes every
where, and where you least expect them, too. She's no glutton, no
drinker, and sound in advice – just look at all the gold. But it's a
wicked tongue she has, the slanderous jay. Whom she loves, she
loves. Whom she doesn't, she doesn't. As for Trimalchio, his real
estate extends as far as the kite flies, with money stacked on money.
He has more silver aside in his porter's lodge than anyone else has to
his name. And his household – why, stone the crows, I swear I don't
believe a tenth of 'em know their own master. In short, he'd fling
any of these monkeys into the cabbage-patch.

'And don't think he goes buying things, either. Everything's on 38
his doorstep. Wool, citrus, pepper; ask him for hen's milk and
you'll see it. For instance, his own wool wasn't good enough for
him; he bought rams in Tarentum, a slap on the rump, and they
were in his flocks. Attic honey now – he had bees fetched from
Athens to produce it on the spot, incidentally rather improving his

domestic stock with these Greeks. Why, in the last few days he has written to have mushroom-spore sent him from India. And, for example, not one of his mules but is born of a wild ass. Just look at all these cushions. Not one that isn't stuffed with purple or scarlet wool. So happy is he! Yet mind you don't turn your nose up at the other freedmen. They're abominably well-off. Look at the one lying on the end of the last couch. At the moment he's worth eight hundred thousand. He rose from the gutter. He used to carry faggots on his back. But by what they say – not that I know, but I have heard – he snatched the cap off a gnome, and unearthed a treasure-hoard.[21] Yet I envy no man if a god gives him something. And he still smarts under his blow of freedom and wills himself no ill. So he has just published this notice: *C. Pompeius Diogenes is letting his lodgings from 1st July. He has bought himself a house.* But what about the one reclining in the freedman's place? What a life he led! He saw his million, but he crashed quite badly, and I don't think there's a hair on his head that isn't pledged. But egud, it's not his fault, there's not a better man, but it's those scoundrels of freedmen who've scoffed the lion's share. Mark my words, when their cauldron goes off the boil, once things go to the bad, it's goodbye to your friends. And the business he was in, so honest, that you should see him come to this! He ran a funeral parlour. He would dine like a king. Boars roasted whole, fantasies in pastry! Game-fowl! Cooks, and pastry-cooks! More wine spilled under his table than anyone else keeps in his cellar! A legend, not a mortal man. When his affairs began to go badly, he was afraid his creditors would twig his embarrassment, and he announced a sale by this poster: *C. Julius Proculus will put up his surplus effects for sale by auction.*

39   Trimalchio interrupted this agreeable table-talk, for the course had been removed, and the guests, now merry with wine, had begun a general conversation.

So Trimalchio, reclining on his elbow, said, 'You have to forge ahead with the wine. Fish have to swim. But I ask you, do you think I'm satisfied with that dish you saw on the stand?

Is this what Ulysses means to you?[22]

Good enough; it does to know one's literature even when dining-out. May the bones of my old patron rest in peace, who would have me be a man of the world. I can be shown nothing new, as that dish has proved. These heavens up here – they are inhabited by twelve gods and turn into as many figures. Then they become a Ram. And whoever is born under that sign has many flocks, many fleeces, a hard head besides, a brazen front, and a sharp horn. The greater part of pedants and pettifoggers is born beneath this sign.'

Praise for our witty astrologer, who goes on: 'Then the whole heavens become a miniature Bull. Under it are born those who kick against the pricks, cattlemen, and those that find their own food. Under the Twins are born team-horses, oxen, great woman-isers, and such as have it both ways. Myself, I was born under the Crab. Therefore I stand on many feet and possess much in the sea and much on land, for your crab's at home both there and here. That's why I've placed nothing over it for some time, for fear of jeopardising my constellation. Gluttons and martinets come into the world under the Lion; women, slaves and runaways under the Virgin; butchers, perfume-sellers and all who weigh out anything under the Balance; poisoners and assassins under the Scorpion. Under the Archer, the cockeyed who squint at the vegetables and lift the bacon fat; the Goat, sad wretches whose misfortunes sprout horns on their heads; the Water-carrier sees taverners and dunder-heads born; caterers and orators come under the Fishes. Thus the circle turns as a millstone, and at every moment some noxious thing is done, that either men die or men are born. As for the sod of turf in the middle and the honeycomb on it, I do nothing without a reason. Mother earth is in the middle, rounded like an egg, and like the honeycomb has all good things in herself.'

'Admirable!' we cried as one man, and raising our hands to the 40 ceiling we swore Hipparchus and Aratus[23] were not to be classed with him. Then servants came in and draped cloths on the couches, which were painted with nets, hunters lying in wait with spears, and the whole armoury of the chase. We could make nothing of this for a while, and then a terrific din was raised outside the dining-room, and here was a pack of Spartan hounds that began to cast round the table. After this came a stand on which was a boar of unsurpassed size wearing a freedman's cap. Two baskets woven of palm-leaves hung down from the tusks, one filled with fresh dates from Syria, one with dried dates from Thebes. Piglets whittled out of cake were spaced about it supposedly taking suck, to show it really was a sow. They were meant to be taken away as presents, too. But to cut up the boar it was not Carver who had carved the fattened fowl that stepped up, but some bearded giant, whose legs were swathed in bindings and who wore a brocade cloak. Drawing a hunting-knife, he struck a violent blow in the flank of the boar. Out of this wound flew thrushes. Fowlers were ready with limed twigs, and in no time at all caught them on the wing as they circled the table. Then, when he had allocated everyone his bird, Trimalchio added, 'Just look what luscious acorns this pig fed on.' At once some boys came up to the baskets hung on the tusks and divided the dry and the sticky dates among the guests.

41   In the meantime, I indulged in private reverie in my quiet corner, and racked my brains to know why the boar had a freedman's cap on his head. After exhausting all my own conjectures, I steeled myself to ask my commentator about what tortured me.

'Why, even your own slave could tell you that,' he said. 'There's no mystery. It's as plain as his face. This boar was relegated to the last course of yesterday's dinner, the guests let him go, and so today he returns to the meal manumitted, as you might say.'

I could have kicked myself for my stupidity, and asked no more questions in case it looked as if I had never dined in good company before.

While we were talking an attractive boy came in. Ivy and vine-leaves were bound round his brow, and as he took round a wicker-basket full of bunches of grapes he professed himself now Bacchus Roaring, now Bacchus Uninhibited, and then Bacchus Crying Joy, and he relayed his master's poems in the shrillest of voices. Trimalchio turned to face this noise. 'Dionysus,' he said, 'be thou free!'

The boy took the cap off the boar's head and put it on his own. And Trimalchio capped that with, 'You won't deny that I have a father who makes free.'[24]

We applauded his *bon mot*, and the boy did the rounds for his customary and fervent kisses. Trimalchio rose from this scene and went to his chamber-pot. Our despot gone, we relaxed and tried to get some conversation going at table. Dama called for a glass and was the first to begin.

'A day is nothing,' he said. 'You turn on your heel, and it's night. So there's nothing better than to go straight from bed to table. And

damned cold it's been too – my bath scarcely warmed me. But a
hot drink's as good as a greatcoat. I've taken it neat and I'm quite
sodden. Wine gone to my head.'

Seleucus joined in.   42

'Myself,' he said, 'I don't wash every day, the masseur beats you
like a fuller. Water has teeth, and every day sees our heart soften in
it. But fortified with a honeyed drink, why, the whores can have
my cold . . . ! But I couldn't have a bath, I was at a funeral today.
Chrysanthus, one of the best, a good fellow, and he gave up the
ghost. Yesterday, yesterday he spoke to me, and I seem to be
talking with him yet. Ah! We pace about like puffed-up bladders,
and are less than the flies. They at least have got something in 'em,
and we are mere bubbles. And suppose he hadn't been on a diet?
For five days, not a drop of water passed his lips, not a crumb of
bread – and yet he's gone to the great majority. It was the doctors
who did for him, or his bad luck rather, for a doctor is nothing
more than a sop to the soul. But he was buried in style on the same
bed he had when he was alive, and with a good pall-cloth. Very
much lamented too, having set free a number of slaves, and it was
only his wife who shed crocodile tears. And what if he hadn't
treated her in the best of ways? For woman as woman is a species of
kite. Nobody ought to do any of 'em any good, it's pouring water
into a well. But old love is an eating canker.'

He was beginning to bore, and Phileros came out with this.   43

'Put in a word for the living! He got what he deserved. He lived
the good life and died an honest death. What's wrong with that?
He was born with a penny and would have bitten a farthing from
a dunghill with his teeth. So he grew up, and it was this way and
that way, just like a honeycomb. Heavens above, I believe he left a
cool hundred thousand and all in coin. But to tell you the truth,
and I have it from the horse's mouth, he was foul-tongued, a
blabberer, he made bad blood, he was no man. His brother was an
excellent fellow, a real friend with an open hand and a slap-up
table. To start with he went through the mill, but the first vintage
put him on his feet again, for he sold as much of his wine as he
wanted to. What kept his chin up was the property he came into
which enabled him to lay hands on more than was left him. And
that dolt, quarrelling with his brother, left his estate to some bastard
or other. He must fly far who shies from his relatives. But he had

slaves he relied on as oracles, and they did him down. A man who trusts too easily will never do well, especially a business man. One thing is certain, he enjoyed his life as long as he was living it. A bird in the hand's worth two in the bush . . . A clear case of being born in the lap of the gods. Lead turned to gold in his grasp. Easy enough, when everything goes on wheels. And how many years do you think he carried off with him? Seventy upwards. But he was hard, he carried his age well, and he was as black as a raven. I knew the man for years and years, always the old rake. No, I'll swear it, I don't think there was a dog in the house he left alone. A great one for the girls, an all-round man. I don't blame him, it was the only thing he took with him.'

44   This was what Phileros said. Then this from Ganymede.

'What he is saying has nothing to do with life, and all this time no one seems to be worried about the gnawing high cost of living. Damn it, I couldn't buy a mouthful of bread today. And the drought goes on and on! There's been famine for a year now. Blast these clerks who are in with the bakers – you scratch my back and I'll scratch yours! The working class sweat because it's carnival every day for these outsize jaws. If only we had the hearties I found here when I first arrived from Asia! That was the life! If the flour wasn't up to standard, they larruped these jumping-jacks so much Jupiter himself might have been envious.

'I remember Safinius. He lived by the Old Arch when I was a boy. A pepper of a man! Wherever he walked he blistered the pavement. But so upright, so sure, a friend to his friends, you could safely play guess-how-many-fingers with him in the dark.[25] You should have seen how he treated them in the Senate-house! He never used figures of speech, but spoke straight to the point. And when he addressed the courts his voice swelled like a trumpet. He never sweated, never spat. I think he had a touch of the Asiatic in him. And so friendly when he greeted you back, calling everyone by his name, just like one of us. Well, at that time the harvest was going dirt cheap. A loaf you paid a farthing for, you couldn't get through it, even with your old woman. Nowadays one bull's eye is bigger. Lord, every day it gets worse! The community grows down and out, like a calf's tail. But why have we got a Town Clerk who's not worth three figs, who prefers a penny in his pocket to our livelihood? He has junketings at home because in one day he gets more cash than the next man will inherit. I know just how he got one lot of a thousand gold pieces! Yet if we were well hung he wouldn't be so cocksure. The people now – lions at home and foxes abroad. As for me, I've eaten my way through my old clothes, and if the high prices persist, I shall sell my hovels. What will happen if neither gods nor men take pity on the town? As truly as I wish to be blessed by my children, I believe it all comes from the gods above. Nobody now believes heaven is heaven, nobody observes the fast, nobody gives a damn for Jupiter, but they all screw up their eyes and reckon the worth of their goods. In the old days women went barefoot to the Capitol, hair dishevelled, pure in heart, and they begged for rain from Jupiter. There and then – then or never at all – it bucketed down, and everybody was happy and as wet as water-rats. I say the gods creep off with muffled feet, because we dissent. The fields lie fallow . . . '

'Cheer up, for goodness' sake,' put in Echion the ragman. It's 45 black spots on white, or white on black, as the yokel said when he lost his brindled pig.[26] What we lack today we get tomorrow. Thus life jogs along. No, by gad, no country could claim to be better, if it only had men in it. We're in trouble in these times, and we're not the only ones. There's no call to be squeamish; there's always a blue sky above. But if you were anywhere else, you'd say that the pigs here walk about ready-roasted. And now we are about to have a first-class three-day show by gladiators, not a professional troop, but freedmen mostly. Our Titus has a large heart and is full of beans; it, will either be this or that, something at any rate. I'm well in with him, you know, and he's no half-and-half fellow. He will provide the best blades and no quarter, and a slaughter-house in the middle so the whole amphitheatre can see. And he has the where-withal. He was left thirty million when his father came to grief. Suppose he spent four hundred thousand, his inheritance wouldn't feel the pinch, and his name will never be forgotten. He has already procured as many toughs as you like, a woman to fight from a chariot, and Glyco's steward, who was surprised in bed with his mistress. You'll see a public brawl between the cuckolds and the cuckold-makers. Anyway, Glyco, a man of no means, turned over his steward to the beasts. Which was as good as exposing himself. How's the servant to blame if his hand is forced? It's his old chamber-pot who's more deserving to be tossed by the bull. Yet

can't get at the ass thrashes the packsaddle. For how could
ɔ imagine that Hermogenes' bad lot could ever come to a
good end? The father was a man to pare the talons of a kite on the
wing, and, well, a snake doesn't hatch a coil of rope. Glyco now,
Glyco got rid of his own daughters, and he will bear the mark as
long as he lives, and only Hell itself shall blot it out. But a man's
mistakes are his own.

'Yet I can smell the kind of feed Mammaea will give us, with two
bits of coin for me and my friends. If he did that he would put
Norbanus in the shade. You must know he will beat him hollow.
And when you get down to it, what good has t'other one done us?
He gave us two twopenny gladiators, now so decrepit they would
fall down if you blew. I've seen better men thrown to the beasts.
The horsemen he had killed, now; they were like mannikins from
oil-lamps, you'd think they were poultry-cocks. One like a loaded
ass, the other bandy-legged, a third replaced a dead 'un and was
near dead himself, and hamstrung too. One of them, a Thracian,
cut a good figure, and fought by the book. To be brief, in the end
they were all sliced about, there were such cries of "Give it 'em!"
from the crowd. Really, they were sheer funks. "All the same," said
he, "I have put on a show." And I applauded you. Add it all up –
I have given you more than I got. One hand washes the other.

46   'Well, Agamemnon, you seem to be saying to me, "What *is* that
boring fellow getting at?" And that is because you who know how
to talk do not talk. You're not one of us and you laugh at what
common folk have to say. We all know that literature has gone to
your head. Well now – one of these days I will get you to come
down to my farm and see my cottages. There'll be something to
eat, a chicken, eggs; it will be a real treat, even if the bad weather
has spoiled everything this year. We'll have all we need to gorge
ourselves on. And then my boy is growing up to be one of your
school. He can already divide by four, and if he lasts you will have
a little slave by your side. Whenever he has a moment to himself
he has his head in a book. He's a good lad, and clever too, but he
has a morbid love of birds. I have had to kill off three goldfinches
already. I said a weasel ate them. But he found other hobbies, and
he's mad about painting. For the rest, he's just begun with Greek
and is getting a fair grasp of Latin, although his master is rather
complacent. And he can never stay put – he is always asking me

for something to read, but won't apply himself. I have another one
too, not very learned, but painstaking, and who teaches more than
he knows. He makes a habit of coming to the house on holidays,
and is happy with whatever you give him. So I bought the boy
some legal digests, for I want him to have a smattering of the law
to be useful about the house. There's daily bread to be won by it.
He's been spattered with literature enough already. If he shies, I'll
have him taught some profession, barber, auctioneer, or at all
events a lawyer, something only death will put a stop to. I din it
into him every day: "Primigenius my boy, believe me, what you
learn is all for yourself. Look at Phileros the lawyer; if he hadn't
studied he wouldn't be able to keep the wolf from the door. Not
so long ago he peddled with a heavy pack on his shoulders, and
now he stands up even to Norbanus. Learning's a treasure, and a
craft lives for ever." '

Talk of this kind was being bandied about when Trimalchio 47
came back. He mopped his brow and washed his hands with
perfume. There was a slight pause.

'Pardon me, my dear friends,' he said, 'but I have been constipated
for several days. My doctors can't make head or tail of it. However,
I have been relieved by a suppository of pomegranate-rind and
pinewood in vinegar. But I hope my stomach will now resume its
old sense of honour. Besides, it rumbles so, anybody would think I
was a bull. So if any of you wants to do his duty, there's nothing to
be ashamed of. Nobody is born perfect. Personally, I don't think
there's a greater torture than holding yourself in. It's the one thing
even Jupiter can't stop. And you laugh at me, Fortunata, you who
keep me wide awake all night? I never deny any man at my tables
the pleasure of doing what he wants, and the doctors don't hold
with retention. If anything urgent crops up, it's all ready outside:
water, chamber-pots, and all the last refinements. Take my word for
it, once the vapours get to your head, they upset the whole body.
I've known many a man die of it through not owning up to himself.'

We gave thanks for his generosity and thoughtfulness, and
swallowed our laughter along with innumerable short drinks. But
we did not realise we were only in the middle of the feast and that
the rest, as they say, was all uphill work. There was music, the
tables were cleared, and into the dining-room they led three white
pigs adorned with muzzles and bells. Their barker said[27] one was

two years old, another three, and the third as much as six. Well, I
thought some acrobats had come in and that the pigs would
perform something rather unusual, as they do in sideshows, but
Trimalchio dashed our hopes by saying, 'Which of them would
you like dished up for dinner at a moment's notice? A fowl, a hash
à la Pentheus, and that sort of miserable thing is all very well for
bumpkins to turn out, but my cooks are used to boiling whole
calves in their coppers.'

And at once he sent for a cook, and without waiting for our
selection told him to slaughter the eldest pig. Then he raised his
voice: 'From which household division are you?'

'From the fortieth,' the man said.

'Purchased, or born here?'

'Neither,' said the cook, 'I was left you in Pansa's will.'

'Well, see you serve it up properly, or I'll have you downgraded
to messenger boy.'

Upon this reminder of the master's power, the meat–dish–to–be
led the cook to the kitchen.

48   To us, Trimalchio turned a milder face, and said, 'If the wine
isn't good enough for you, I'll get some different. It's up to you to
give it a good name. Glory be, I don't have to buy it. Nowadays
everything to make the mouth water comes up on one of my
estates, one I know nothing of so far. They say it borders on
Tarracina and Tarentum.[28] What I do want to do now is join
Sicily to my pieces of land, so if I fancy going to Africa, I can cross
over by my own territory. But tell me, Agamemnon, what issue
did you speak on today? I don't plead cases myself, but I have got
up literature for private purposes. And don't think I look down
my nose on learning; I have two libraries, one Greek and another
one Latin. So tell me the gist of your speech, there's a good
fellow.'

Agamemnon began: 'A poor man and a rich man were once at
odds.'

'What,' said Trimalchio, 'is a poor man?'

'Delightful,' murmured Agamemnon, and went on to expound
an obscure controversy.[29]

But as quick as anything, Trimalchio took him up: 'If it's a fact,
there's no point at issue; if it isn't a fact, there's nothing there at
all.'

We greeted this and other bright remarks with the most lavish praise.

'My dear Agamemnon, do tell me,' he went on, 'do you remember anything of the twelve labours of Hercules, or the story of Ulysses, and how the Cyclops twisted his thumb with the tongs?[30] I used to read about it myself in Homer when I was a boy. And the Sybil, of course. I saw her hanging in a bottle at Cumae[31] with my own eyes, and when the lads asked, "Sybil, what do you want?" she would answer, "I want to die." '

He was still prattling on when in came a dish with a huge pig on 49 it. It covered the whole table. We admired the cook's speed, and swore not even a fowl could have been prepared so swiftly, especially as the pig seemed considerably larger than the boar had been a short time back. Trimalchio's eyes grew wider and wider and he said, 'What? What? The pig's not been gutted? Nor has it. Call him on! Call on the cook!'

The cook came up to the table with a long face and said he had forgotten to gut the animal.

'What do you mean, forgotten?' roared Trimalchio. 'As much as to say he never handled pepper and cummin! Off with his things!'

In a trice the cook was stripped and stood woefully flanked by two bullies. We all began to put in a good word for him and say, 'This sort of thing *will* happen; do let him off; if he does it again, we won't stand by him.'

I couldn't help myself; with a complete lack of feeling, I leaned over and said grimly in Agamemnon's ear, 'Really, this servant must be quite impossible. Forget to clean out a pig! I swear I wouldn't even let him off if he had done it with a mere fish!'

But Trimalchio's face had softened and was all smiles.

'Oh well,' he said, 'since your memory is going, gut him here in front of us.'

The cook put his shirt on, seized his knife and discreetly slit the pig's belly in one or two places. A second later the cuts widened under inside pressure and out came tumbling sausages and blood-puddings.

At this the servants all burst into well-drilled applause, and 50 shouted as with one voice, 'Good luck to Gaius!' The cook too was rewarded with a silver crown and a drink from a cup served on a Corinthian plate. When Agamemnon looked at it rather intently,

Trimalchio announced, 'I am the only man to possess genuine Corinthian ware.'

I was waiting for him to say with his usual self-conceit that he imported his dishes from Corinth itself. But he went one better.

'Perhaps,' he said, 'you would like to know why I alone have the real Corinthian. Quite simply, the name of the maker I buy them from is Corinthus. What can be called Corinthian if it's not what comes from Corinthus? And don't go thinking I'm a bloody fool. I know very well the origin of Corinthian stuff. When Ilium fell, Hannibal,[32] that insidious man, that king-chameleon, heaped all the bronze statues and the gold ones and the silver ones in one pile and set fire to the lot. They melted into a single metal alloy. So all the casters took from this mass and made plates and dishes and statuettes. That's how Corinthian things came about, something of everything in one, neither flesh nor fowl. But forgive me if I say I myself prefer glass, which at least has no odour. If it weren't so fragile I would prefer it to gold; but it's poor stuff these days. Yet
51 there was once a glazier who made an unbreakable glass cup. With this gift he got audience with Caesar; he made him hand it back and then he dashed it on the floor. Caesar was terrified out of his wits. But the man picked up the cup from the ground – dented, like a bronze dish. Then he whipped out a tiny hammer from his pocket and tapped it back into true without the least fuss. After this, he thought he had Jupiter himself by the short and curly, especially when the Emperor asked him, "Does anyone else know how to make glass this way?" Just wait though. When he said no, Caesar had him beheaded, for if his secret were ever out, gold
52 would go dirt cheap. But I am a great connoisseur of silver myself. I have roughly a hundred tankards of large capacity decorated with how Cassandra killed her children, and their bodies lying there quite lifelike. I have a jug left me by one of my patrons on which Daedalus shuts Niobe in the Trojan horse. I have the combats of Hermeros and Petraites[33] on my cups, all heavy stuff; I wouldn't sell my knowledge of these things at any price.'

A boy dropped a cup while he was talking. Trimalchio turned to look at him and say: 'Quick, go and take your own head off, since you are so dim-witted.'

The boy's lip trembled and he started to plead.

'Why ask me?' said Trimalchio. 'As if I wanted to hurt you! My advice to you is watch yourself and don't be silly.'

In the end we won him over and he let the boy go. As soon as he was free, he began running round the table. And he cried out, 'Off with the water, on with the wine.' We took up this pleasantry, Agamemnon ahead of all, for he knew on what score a man is invited out again. Heaped with our praises, Trimalchio drank, beaming all over. Drunkenness was creeping up on him.

'None of you,' he said, 'asking my Fortunata to dance? Believe me, she does a first-class *cordax*.'[34]

He raised his hands about his face and gave an imitation of the actor Syrus, while the whole household chanted: '*Medeia perimadeia!*'[35] He would have come right out in the middle if Fortunata had not whispered something in his ear, probably that such common clowning ill suited his dignity. But then nothing was so variable as his mood; there were times when he respected his Fortunata, and times when he reverted to his old self. But his desire to caper was utterly quashed by a clerk who read out loud, as if from the *Roman Gazette*, 'July 26th. On Trimalchio's estate at Cumae thirty boys and forty girls were born. Five hundred thousand pecks of wheat were taken from the threshing-floor to the granary. Five hundred oxen were broken in. The same day the slave Mithridates was crucified for slandering the genius of our Gaius. The same day ten millions were relegated to the strong-box for lack of suitable investments. The same day fire broke out in the Pompeian gardens, beginning in the house of Nasta the estate manager.'

'Eh?' said Trimalchio. 'When did I buy the Pompeian gardens?'

'Last year,' said the clerk, 'and that's why they haven't been entered in the accounts yet.'

Trimalchio exploded with rage. 'Whatever properties are bought for me,' he said, 'if I don't know about them in six months, I won't have them put to my account.'

We now heard public notices read out, and the wills of foresters, from which Trimalchio was cut out by a special clause; then a list of farmers, the name of the freedwoman divorced by a night watchman on being caught in the act with a bathing-attendant, the name of a major domo banished to Baiae,[36] the arraignment of a treasurer, and the verdict in an action between a number of valets.

At last the acrobats made an entry. A clod of exceptional dullness stood up with a ladder and ordered a boy to dance up every rung and sing at the top. Then he had to jump through burning hoops and lift a jar with his teeth. Trimalchio was the only one to admire this performance, and he would keep saying it was a thankless profession, but there were only two things in the whole world he watched with pleasure, acrobats and horn-blowers. All the rest, animals, comic turns, was pure trash.

'You see,' he added, 'I did buy some classic comedians, but I preferred them doing local farces, and I had my flautist play Latin tunes.'

54   At this point in his conversation the boy fell on top of Trimalchio. The servants let out a cry, and the guests too, not because of this putrid character whose neck they would have gladly seen broken, but for fear of its bringing the feast to a disastrous end, and their having to bewail a death that was nothing to them. As for Trimalchio, he let out a deep groan and nursed one arm as if injured. Doctors rushed up, headed by Fortunata, her hair flying and a draught-cup in her hand. She gave voice to her misery and hapless plight. And the boy who fell had now been grovelling at our feet for some time, and he implored our pardon. My worst fear was that his soliciting was really a hoax leading up to some *coup de théâtre*. That cook who forgot to gut the pig was still in my mind. So I began to look all round the room in case an automaton sprang out of the wall, especially when I saw a slave beaten for dressing his master's bruised arm in white rather than purple wool. My suspicions were not far out. Instead of punishment there came Trimalchio's decision to set the boy free, so that nobody could say
55   so illustrious a man had been wounded by a slave. We showed our wholehearted approval of this action, and we buzzed with various phrases about how uncertain life was.

'Surely,' said Trimalchio, 'we shouldn't let the event slip by without a record.'

There and then he asked for a writing-tablet, and without straining his mental faculties overmuch recited these hobbling verses:

> Things come by contraries, unexpected,
> And Fortune ministers above our heads.
> So top us up with Falernian, boy.

This epigram introduced the question of poetry. For a considerable time it was argued that the peak of lyricism was the domain of Mopsus of Thrace,[37] until Trimalchio said, 'Now I ask you, scholar that you are, how would you distinguish between Cicero and Publilius?[38] I myself think one was more eloquent, and the other more elevated. What can you quote that's better than this?

> Rome's ramparts tumble in the abyss of pleasure.
> For you to taste the caged peacock is crammed,
> Wrapped in feathers like Babylonian cloth of gold,
> The guinea fowl, and the capon too.
> Even the stork, that welcome traveller,
> Model of filial piety, slender-legged, rattle-voiced,
> Winter's exiled bird, who warns of warmer days,
> Now nests in your damned stewpot.
> What's a priceless pearl, India's fruit, to you?
> That your wife all jewelled with sea-treasures
> Collapses frantic on the stranger's bed?
> What use the green emerald, that precious glass,
> Or gleam thrown by the stones of Carthage,
> Unless honesty shines from these carbuncles?
> Is it right for a bride to wear wind-like gauze,
> And come naked in public clouded in muslin?

'Yet what do you think,' he went on, 'is the most difficult 56 profession after writing? Well, to my mind a doctor's or a money-changer's. The doctor, because he knows what we poor fellows have in our insides, and when a fever is coming up – although I particularly loathe those of 'em who are always making me eat duck – and the money-changer for seeing the copper beneath the silver. You see, oxen and sheep are the hardest-working among dumb animals; oxen, whose labour gives us bread to eat, sheep, because we can cut such a dash in clothes of their wool. And it's a crying shame that people eat lamb and wear woollen shirts too. Bees now, I think they're divine creatures, they spew honey, although some say they bring it from Jupiter. They sting too, and that's because wherever a sweet thing is you will find something bitter too.'

He was by way of throwing the philosophers out of work when tickets were passed round in a cup. The boy charged with this duty read out the punning list of presents.

'Criminal silver!' They fetched a ham with a vinegar-bottle on top.

'A pillow for the neck!' It was a bit of neck-beef.

'Belated wisdom and dumb insolence!' This one got dry salt biscuits and a stick with an apple.

'Leeks and peaches!' He had a whip and a knife.

'Sparrows and a fly-flap!' And it was a bunch of dried grapes and some Attic honey.

'Evening-dress and city clothes!' He got a cut of meat and writing-tablets.

'Canal and foot-gauge!' They brought a hare and a slipper.

'Marbled eel and letter!' It was a mouse tied to a frog and a bundle of beetroot. We couldn't stop laughing. There were hundreds of these puns, which escape me now.

57   Ascyltus let himself go to extremes, tossed his hands, parodied everything, and laughed until he cried. One of Trimalchio's fellow-freedmen, seated just above me, was exasperated.

'What are you laughing at, mutton-head?' he cried. 'Don't my master's luxuries suit your taste? I suppose you're better off up at your place and used to the high life. The spirit of the place protect me, but if I were sitting next to him I'd have gagged his bleating by now. What a nob, laughing at the others! Some fly-by-night not worth his own water. To put it precisely, if I pissed all round him, he wouldn't know which way to turn. Strike me, I don't anger easily, but sleepy flesh breeds worms. He laughs! And for what does he laugh? His father bought the baby for gold, did he? You're a Roman knight? I'm a king's son, I am. "Why have you been in service?" you ask. Because I put myself in it and would rather be a Roman citizen than a provincial taxpayer. And now I hope to live so that nobody pokes fun at me. I am a man among men, I go about with my head uncovered, I don't owe a brass farthing, I've never been had up for anything, nobody's said to me on 'change, "Pay up your debts." I bought some pieces of land, scraped in some pennies; I have twenty bellies to fill and a dog; I ransomed my fellow-slave to stop 'em wiping their hands on her; I paid a thousand for my own head; I was made Augustan priest free of charge; and if I die, I hope I may have nothing to blush for when I'm dead. But you! So busy you can't look behind you? You see the lice on others but not the ticks on yourself. We're ridiculous only to you. Look at your tutor, a grown-up man; now, *he* likes us. You're still at the breast, you can't pipe "mu" or "ma", you clay-pot, yes, a wash-leather in water, softer, but none the better for it. You're richer! Well, have *two* breakfasts, *two* dinners. I prefer my repute to any money. Put it like this: who ever had to call for me twice? Forty years in service, and nobody ever knew if I was a slave or free. I was a long-haired chit when I came to these parts: they hadn't built the municipal hall then. I worked hard to please my master, a real gentleman, a swell, and his little finger was worth more than the whole of you. And there were some in the house always ready to trip me up now and then, but – thanks to the master – I won through. There's real victories for you; as for being born free, it's as easy as saying "Come here." But why gape at me like a goat stuck in a vetch-field?'

At this Giton, who was at our feet and had been holding himself 58 in for some time, burst out with a disgraceful laugh. This did not escape Ascyltus' inquisitor, who now turned to harangue the boy.

'You too, laughing, you frizzled onion? Carnival time, eh? I put it to you, is this the month of December? When did you pay off your five per cent for freedom?[39] And what's he going to do, the gallows-tripe, the crow's carrion? And now I'm going to bring down the wrath of Jupiter on you and the other one who can't keep you in your place. As I'm stuffed with bread, it's only out of regard for my fellows that I don't, else I would have settled it with you. Here we are enjoying ourselves, then we get dunderheads who can't keep you in hand. That's it – like master, like man. I'm nearly bursting, but I'm not hot-headed by nature. But once I start, I wouldn't give two kicks for my own mother. All right then – I shall meet you in the street, you rat, you puff-ball. And I won't be a whit taller or shorter until I've squashed your master beneath a cabbage-leaf. Not sparing you, however much you call on Jupiter in Olympus, no, by all that's mighty. You'll see what your fourpenny kiss-curls and your twopenny master are worth. Right you are, I'll get my teeth into you, and either I don't know myself, or you won't mock me again, even if you get a beard of pure gold. I'll fetch the wrath of Athena down on you and the man who first made you a lickspittle. I didn't learn geometry and criticism and all that nonsense, but I know my capital letters and do money sums and weights and measures. Look, if you like, we'll have a bet. Come on, I've put down my stake. I will prove that your father wasted his money on you even if you do know rhetoric. Ready? What part of us am I? I come from far, I come from wide. Find me.

I can tell you what part of us runs and stays still, and what part of us grows and gets less. Aha! You start, you boggle! You're all over yourself, like a mouse in a chamber-pot. So just keep quiet and don't annoy your better who didn't know you were come into the world. Or did you fancy I cared for those yellow wood-shaving curls you stole from your girlfriend? Occupo help me! Let's go on 'change and raise a loan. You'll see my iron ring gets credit. Oh, and a soaking-wet fox is a very fine sight! As I hope to make my pile, as I hope to die in style, and have 'em swear by my dying day, I'll hound you out with a death-warrant in my hand. An admirable fellow he was whoever taught you, a real mutt, not a teacher. In my day we were taught differently, and our master would say, "Everything shipshape? Then straight home, don't look round, and respect your elders." Now they're all pure humbugs. Not one of them worth twopence. Thank God my education has made me what I am today.'

59 Ascyltus was about to reply to this string of abuse when Trimalchio, who was delighted with his outspoken colleague, said, 'Now stop this savaging. Gently does it, and Hermeros, don't be hard on the youngster. Your blood is hot, but just be the more civil. In this sort of thing it's always the loser who really comes out on top. And you, when you were a young cock, it was all cockadoodledoo, and you were cock-brained too. The best thing is somehow to get back to the fun again, and watch the Homeric actors.'[40]

In came a troop of players and immediately clashed their spears on their shields. Trimalchio sat on a cushion and droned a Latin text while the Homerists conversed in Greek, as is their abominable practice. Soon he called a halt and said, 'Do you know what story they're doing?[41] Diomede and Ganymede were two brothers. Their sister was Helen. Agamemnon carried her off and fooled Diana by sacrificing a deer. That's how Homer is now telling the tale of the war between the Trojans and the Parentines. Of course he won and married Iphigenia his daughter to Achilles. Which is why Ajax went mad, and he will carry on with the story now.'

As Trimalchio spoke the Homerists gave a shout, and amid the

scurrying servants a dish was brought in that was a good two
hundred pounds in weight, and on it a boiled calf, with a helmet on
its head too. Ajax followed with drawn sword and hacked it as if
frenzied. He pranced about with cut and thrust, then collected
titbits on the point of his sword and shared out the carcass among
the astonished guests.

We had little time to admire such far-fetched exhibitions, for 60
suddenly the ceiling resounded and the whole room shook. I rose
in alarm, fearing some acrobat would come through the roof. The
other guests were no less amazed and raised their eyes to whatever
novelty the heavens promised. All at once the ceiling opened and
they lowered an immense hoop, apparently prised off a huge vat.
Golden crowns and jars of ointment hung the whole way round.
While we were being requested to take these presents, I had a look
at the table. A plate with a variety of cakes had already been set
there, and in the middle stood a pastry Priapus with all kinds of
apples and grapes gathered into his fairly ample lap in conventional
style. Greedily we reached out to this display, when suddenly a
new set of pranks set us off again. For every single one of the cakes
and apples, however lightly handled, spurted saffron-water, and
the odious liquid shot all over us. We were convinced that a dish
on which such ceremonial pomp had been lavished must be sacred,
so we all rose up and cried, 'Long live Augustus, the father of his
country.'

Even after this reverent act, some of the guests grabbed at the
apples, so we filled our napkins too, I especially, as I thought I could
never swell Giton's pockets with anything adequate enough.

Meanwhile three boys entered wearing white tucked-up tunics.
Two of them put on the table images of the Lares[42] with golden
lockets, and the third offered round a bowl of wine, crying, 'The
gods be good to us!'

Trimalchio said one was called Profit, another Fortune, and the
third Gain. And as for Trimalchio's own true image, when everybody else kissed it, we were too ashamed to pass it by.

So when they had all wished themselves good health in body and 61
mind, Trimalchio turned to Niceros and said, 'You're usually
more agreeable at table; I don't know why you're silent now, not
uttering a word. Do me a favour, please tell us the adventure that
happened to you.'

Niceros was delighted with his affable companion. 'May every penny of profit slip through my hands,' he replied, 'if I'm not beside myself with joy to see you in such high humour. And so it shall be for a laugh and nothing else, although I'm afraid your pedants may laugh on their side. Let them — I'll get on with my story all the same. What have I got to lose if they laugh at me? Better be laughed at than sneered at.' Thus he spake,[43] and began the following tale.

'When I was still a slave, we lived in a narrow street, in a house that is now Gavilla's. There, by the grace of the gods, I fell in love with the wife of Terentius, the publican; you know, Melissa of Tarentum, a real bit of beauty. But I swear it wasn't her physique or because we made love, but it was more her generous nature. I could ask her anything, and she would never say no; if she made a penny, I got a halfpenny; I handed everything over to her pocket and wasn't cheated of a thing. Well, her husband breathed his last out in the country. So I took my shield and buckled on my greaves, and puzzled out how I might reach her; as the saying goes, friends turn up just when you need them. As luck would have it, my master had gone to Capua to sell some tawdry junk. I seized the opportunity and persuaded a guest to come the five miles with me. He was a soldier, and as brave as hell. We sheered off about cockcrow, and the moon shone as bright as midday. We were passing through some tombstones, and my man busied himself among the epitaphs; I sat down, hummed a little and counted the graves. When I looked round at him, he was stripping and putting his entire clothes by the roadside. My heart was in my mouth, and I stood stock-still. But he just piddled all round his clothes and suddenly turned into a wolf. No joking; I wouldn't lie for all the gold in the world. But as I was about to say, after he had turned into a wolf he began to howl and made for the woods. Me, at first I didn't know which way to look; then I went to pick up his clothes, but they had turned to stone. If ever any man was likely to die of fright it was me. I drew my sword and cut at every shadow, all the way until I reached my mistress's farmhouse. I went in like a corpse, I nearly gave up the ghost, sweat coursed down my thighs, my eyes were blank, and nothing would revive me. My Melissa was surprised to see me about so late, and said, "If you had come earlier you could at least have lent us a hand; a wolf came on

62

the farm and bled all the sheep like a butcher. But he didn't fool me, even though he got away; one of our slaves put a spear through his neck." Hearing this, I could close my eyes no more, and at daybreak I sped like a ransacked vintner back to our master Gaius' house. When I reached the place where the clothes had petrified, I found nothing but blood. Yet when I got home, my soldier was there lying groaning like an ox, in bed, with a doctor tending his neck. Then I knew he was a werewolf, and from that moment I could never break bread with him, not if you held a knife at my throat. They can say what they like about this, and if I lie, may your guardian spirits strike me.'

We were all stunned, but Trimalchio went on, 'I'm not dispar- 63 aging your story; believe me, my hair stood on end. I know Niceros never tells old wives' tales; he's reliable and doesn't talk big. Now I'm going to tell you something to make your flesh creep. Like the case of the ass on the roof-tops.[44] When I still had my curly hair, for I led a sybarite's life from boyhood up, my master's favourite died. There was a pearl for you, in a class of his own, one in a million! His poor mother wept for him, and several of us were there sharing her grief, when suddenly the witches began to screech; it was like a hound on the tail of a hare. At that time we had with us a Cappadocian, a strapping great fellow, fearless and tough. He could pick up a mad bull. He drew his sword and rushed bravely out of doors, his left hand carefully wrapped up, and ran a woman right through the middle, about here where my finger is, and may the gods preserve the spot! We heard a groan, but to tell the truth, we didn't see the witches themselves. Our strong man came back and dropped on the bed. His body was black and blue all over as if he had been flogged, evidently because some evil hand had set about him. We shut the door and returned to our vigil, but when the mother threw herself on the body of her son, she felt only a manikin made of straw. It had no heart, no intestines, no anything; for the witches had stolen the child and left a puppet of straw. You must believe me, I beg you, there are women who know that something extra, and there are those who ride by night and turn things upside down. As for our big tough, he never got his colour back after this, and a few days later he died raving mad.'

We were all wonder and credulity and, kissing the board, we 64 prayed the night-riders to stay home while we returned from dinner.

I must confess that by now the lamps were multiplying before my very eyes, and the whole room was changing, when Trimalchio said, 'Now Plocamus, nothing to say for yourself? Nothing amusing? You used to be so agreeable and recite us scenes from the plays so well, and throw in a song too. Lord, lord, the sweet young figs are over!'

'True,' he replied, 'I've had to use the curb and bit since I was seized with gout. On the other hand I nearly got consumption through singing so much when I was young. And how I danced, and played comedies, how I took off the barbers! When was there anyone my equal, except the inimitable Apelles?'[45]

And putting his hand to his mouth he whistled something foul and unrecognisable which he later pretended was Greek.

Trimalchio would not be outdone. He imitated a trumpet, then leered round at his pet, whom he called Croesus. This was a bleary boy with putrid teeth who was tying a green bandage round a black puppy, an indecently fat one. He had put half a loaf on a cushion and was forcing it down her throat. The bitch refused it and puked. This kindness gave Trimalchio an idea, and he ordered them to fetch Scylax,[46] 'guardian of the house and the household'. Instantly an enormous dog was led in on a chain, and on a hint from the porter's foot to lie down, stretched out before the table. Trimalchio tossed him a bit of white bread with the words, 'Nobody in my house loves me more.'

The boy was piqued by this extravagant praise of Scylax and put his puppy down, encouraging her to get into a fight. True to his doggish nature, Scylax filled the dining-room with a most hideous barking, and nearly tore Croesus's Margarita to pieces. The uproar was not confined to this scrap; a lamp was overturned on the table and shattered all the glassware, and burning oil was splashed on some of the guests. Anxious not to seem upset over this loss, Trimalchio kissed his pet and told him to clamber on his back. He mounted his cock-horse at once and smacked away at Trimalchio's shoulders with his open hand, crying out between laughter, 'Hey cockalorum, how many are we?'[47]

After a while Trimalchio calmed down and ordered a large bowl of wine to be mixed, and had drinks served among all the slaves who

were sitting at our feet. He made this condition: 'If anyone refuses it,
pour it over his head. Business the livelong day, but now for gaiety!'

His show of goodwill was followed by some delicacies the very 65
memory of which, if you can believe me, still turns my stomach.
Each of us had a fat chicken brought him instead of a thrush, and
goose eggs in little caps, which Trimalchio urged us most emphati-
cally to swallow, saying that they were boneless chickens.
Meanwhile an attendant knocked on the dining-room door, and a
reveller dressed in white came in with a large party. I was terrified
by his majestic bearing and took him for the Mayor. So I tried to
get up and set my bare feet on the ground. Agamemnon laughed at
my flurry.

'Whoa, steady, you idiot,' he said. 'It's Habinnas from the
Priests' College,[48] he's a stonemason too, everybody knows his
superior tombstones.'

These words reassured me, and I leaned back to contemplate
Habinnas' entry with considerable amazement. The man was
already drunk, and draped his arms over his wife's shoulders. He
wore several garlands, and some ointment trickled down his
forehead into his eyes. He took the seat of honour and called for
wine and hot water right away. Trimalchio was pleased with his
good humour and ordered a larger cup for himself, and asked him
how he had been received.

'We had everything but you,' was the reply, 'for my mind's eye
was here. But I must say it came off well. Scissa was having her
ninth-day funeral party for her wretched slave. She set him free on
his deathbed. And I rather think she will have an exorbitant sum to
pay in manumission dues; they value the deceased at fifty thousand.
Yet it was all very fine, even if we were obliged to pour half our
drinks over his poor old bones.'

'Yes,' said Trimalchio, 'but what did you have to eat?'

'I'll tell you if I can,' replied the other, 'but my memory is so good 66
I often forget my own name. Well, first of all we had a pig crowned
with a cup, and round it sausages and liver very well done, some
beetroot of course, wholemeal bread baked at home, which I prefer
to white, because it builds you up, and it makes me do my duty
without tears. Then came a dish of cold tart and vintage Spanish
wine poured over warm honey. I didn't touch a bit of tart, but I
gorged myself on the honey. Chickpeas and lupins came round, nuts

to choice and an apple apiece. I lifted two of them myself, and here
they are wrapped in my napkin. There would be trouble if I didn't
bring my little slave a present. Ah! My wife has just reminded me –
we had a portion of bear on display. Scintilla was rash enough to try
some, and she nearly brought up her insides. Yet I guzzled over a
pound of it myself, for it smacked of real wild boar. What I say is,
when the bear devours puny man, the more our puny man ought to
eat up the bear. To round it off we had cream cheese and boiled
wine, every man his snail, bits of tripe, livers on tiny plates, capped
eggs, turnips, mustard, a plate of muck – whoa, Palamedes![49] They
brought round a bowl of cummin in vinegar, and some were
67 perverse enough to take three handfuls. We had waved the ham
aside. But, Gaius, tell me please; why isn't Fortunata at table?'

'You know her well enough,' replied Trimalchio, 'and not a
drop of water passes her lips until she has locked up the silver and
shared out the remains among the slaves.'

'Oh well,' rejoined Habinnas, 'if she doesn't come and sit down,
I'll push off.'

He was getting up when, on a signal, all the servants called out
'Fortunata' four times and more. So in she came, her dress so held
up by a pale green waistband that a cherry-red petticoat could be
seen underneath. She had twisted anklets and white slippers em-
broidered with gold. She wiped her hands on a handkerchief she
had round her neck, and then sat on the sofa where Habinnas' wife
Scintilla was lying. She kissed her as she was clapping her hands and
said, 'Is it really you at last?'

It got to the point where Fortunata took the bracelets off her
podgy arms and flourished them for Scintilla to admire. She went so
far as to undo her anklets and gold hairnet, saying they were pure
quality. Trimalchio saw this happen and ordered it all to be brought
to him.

'Here we have,' he said, 'a woman's shackles, and that's how we
poor dolts are cleaned out. She must have six and a half pounds of
it. Well, I possess a bracelet weighing not a fraction under ten
pounds, made out of the thousandth parts that I owe Mercury.'[50]

In the end, so we could see he did not lie, he had scales brought,
and the weight was proved by their being shown round. Scintilla
was just as bad, and took from her neck a little gold box which she
called her lucky charm. Then she produced two earrings and gave

them to Fortunata to look at in her turn, and said, 'They're a present from my husband, and nobody has any finer.'

'What?' said Habinnas. 'I've been gutted buying you these glass beans. Really, if I had a daughter I would cut her ears off. If there were no women everything would be dirtcheap, but this is pissing warm and drinking cold.'

Meanwhile the fuddled women were giggling at each other and exchanged drunken kisses, and while one boasted of her thrifty housekeeping, the other harped on her husband's favourites and his indifference to her. They were getting together when Habinnas rose on the sly, seized Fortunata by the legs and dumped her on the couch.

'Ooh! Ow!' she shouted as her dress flew above her knees. She righted herself, rushed into Scintilla's arms, and hid her blazing red face in her handkerchief.

Some time passed before Trimalchio ordered the next service of 68 food. The slaves took all the tables away, brought others, scattered sawdust that had been dyed yellow and vermilion and, something new to my eyes, flakes of flittering selenite. Right away Trimalchio said, 'I could be satisfied with this course, for you have had your second service.[51] If there's anything good, bring it on!'

In the meantime a boy from Alexandria, who took round hot water, began to imitate the nightingale, while Trimalchio called out, 'Enough of that!'

Then there was another joke. The slave seated at Habinnas' feet suddenly, but on order I suppose, began to declaim in a singsong voice:

Now Aeneas and his fleet had put to sea . . . [52]

No more excruciating sound ever pierced my ears, for not content with raising or lowering his voice as the barbaric whim took him, he mixed in dirty Atellane verses.[53] For the first time in my life Virgil displeased me. When at last he left off in weariness, Habinnas added, 'He never had any schooling. But I trained him by sending him out with the mountebanks. Nobody can touch him when it comes to imitating mule-drivers or quacks. He's desperately clever; a cobbler, a cook, a pastry-maker, a jack-of-all-trades. But he has two defects, without which he would be perfect: he is circumcised and he snores. I don't mind his squint; Venus

herself was swivel-eyed. That's why he can't keep quiet, his eye is
never out of action. He cost me three hundred . . . '

69   Scintilla interrupted what he was saying: 'It seems to me you are
not telling all the accomplishments of your nasty slave. He's your
pimp, and I'll see he's branded for it.'

Trimalchio laughed.

'I can sense the Cappadocian in him,' he said. 'He does himself
out of nothing and, damn it all, he has my approval. It's not the sort
of thing you get offered when you're dead. You, Scintilla, don't be
jealous. We know what women are, believe me. Bless my soul, I
used to go in for horseplay with my mistress until my master grew
suspicious and banished me to a country estate. But hush, my
tongue, and you'll have some bread.'

Supposing this to be praise, the abominable slave drew a clay
lamp out of his dress and imitated trumpeters for over half an hour,
and Habinnas droned an accompaniment, his fingers pressed on his
lower lip. Finally he came into the middle of the floor, and first
with a few broken reeds imitated the flute-players and then, with a
whip and a weatherproof, gave us *The Muleteer's Life*,[54] until
Habinnas called him over and kissed him. He offered him a drink
and said, 'Better and better, Massa – I'll give you some boots.'

We should never have seen the end of these mediocrities if the last
course had not been served, thrushes rolled in wheaten flour and
stuffed with nuts and raisins. To follow, quinces stuck with prickles
to look like sea-urchins. This could have been tolerated if a far more
preposterous dish had not compelled us to prefer death by starvation. When set down, it was, or so we thought, a fattened goose
with fish and miscellaneous birds round it . . . said Trimalchio:
'Whatever you see before you is made out of one substance.'

I, of course, in my worldly wisdom, knew what it was at once,
and turning to Agamemnon I said, 'What the whole thing is made
of doesn't surprise me in the least. Or it could be mud: I've seen
faked-up dinners of this kind at Rome during Carnival.'

70   Before I had finished speaking, Trimalchio went on to say, 'As I
hope to increase in wealth and not round the waist, my cook has
made the whole show out of a pig. There couldn't be a more
valuable fellow. Would you believe it, he makes a fish out of the
womb; a pigeon out of bacon, a turtledove of the ham, and a
chicken of the knuckle-end. And they have given him a very fine

name of my own invention; he is called Daedalus.[55] I brought him some knives of Noricum steel back from Rome, a present because he is so gifted.'

He had these knives produced at once and looked them over in admiration. He even let us try the edge on our cheeks.

Suddenly two slaves came in who seemed to have been squabbling by the cistern; at least they had their pitchers on their shoulders. When Trimalchio wanted to settle their quarrel, neither would accept his judgement, but each smashed the other's pitcher with his stick. We were startled by the insolence of these drunkards and stared at their battle, only to see cockles and mussels tumble from the pitchers, and a boy pick them up on a plate, which he took round. Our precious cook was fully equal to this refinement, he offered us snails on a silver grid, and sang a song in a foul tremolo.

I blush to tell what happened next. In an unheard-of way, long-haired boys brought an ointment in a silver basin and anointed our feet as we lay there, first binding garlands round our feet and ankles. Then some of the same ointment was poured into the wine-bowl and the lamp.

Already Fortunata made as if to dance, and already Scintilla applauded more spontaneously than she spoke, when Trimalchio said, 'You, Philargyrus, and you, Cario, though a notorious partisan of the Greens,[56] I permit you to sit down, and tell your woman Menophila to do the same.'

Need I say more? We were nearly thrown off our sofas as the slaves invaded every corner of the room. I for one noticed just above me the cook who had made a goose of a pig, and he stank of pickle and sauce. Having a seat was not enough for him; right away he started to imitate the tragedian Ephesus[57] and then bet his own master that the Greens would carry off first prize at the next games. This challenge put Trimalchio in an expansive mood.

'My friends,' he said, 'slaves are men just like we are, and they drank their mothers' milk like one of us even if they have been oppressed by an evil fate. But soon they shall drink of the waters of freedom, and in my lifetime too. The truth is, I am setting them all free in my will. I am leaving Philargyrus some land and his woman too, and equally Cario gets a block of tenements, the price of his freedom, and a bed and some bedding. My dear Fortunata is to be my heir, and I recommend her to all my friends. All of which I make public so that the household may love me now as if I were already dead.'

They began to give thanks to their master for his generosity, and then he took the thing in earnest, had a copy of the will brought up, and read it all from beginning to end while the whole gathering groaned.

He turned to face Habinnas: 'Tell me, my good friend, are you going to erect me a monument as I ordered? I do most sincerely beg you to carve my little bitch at the foot of my statue, with wreaths and jars of perfume, and the complete fights of Petraites, so that thanks to you I shall live after I am dead. And the whole thing to have a frontage of one hundred feet, a depth of two hundred feet. You see, I want all kinds of fruit growing round my ashes, with plenty of vines. It is completely misguided to decorate your house while you are alive and do nothing about the home you will live in so much longer. For this reason I want this to be added on, above all: "This monument is no part of my legacy." What is more, I shall take good care to provide in my will against injury after death. I shall appoint a freedman to be guardian of my tomb to stop the rabble running up to befoul it. And please carve me ships in full sail on my tomb, and myself sitting in robes on my official seat, five gold rings on my fingers, distributing money to the people from a bag; you remember I gave a free dinner and two silver coins a head. If you can possibly manage, I should like the dining-room done as well, with all the people doing themselves proud. On my right hand put a statue of Fortunata holding a dove with a bitch on a leash, and my white-headed boy, and enormous wine-jars, well sealed-up, so that nothing spills. And carve a broken urn with a boy weeping over it. A clock in the middle so that whoever looks at the time will read my name whether he wants to or no. As for the epitaph go over this carefully and see if you think it will do:

Here lies GAIUS POMPEIUS TRIMALCHIO from
Maecenas' house. The rank of Priest of Augustus was
conferred on him in his absence. He could have been in
any Public Service, but refused. Pious, valiant, a man of
his word, he rose from nothing and left thirty million.
He never listened to a philosopher.
God bless him. And bless you too.'

When he finished this, Trimalchio burst into a flood of tears, 72
Fortunata wept, Habinnas wept, and the whole household filled
the room with lamentation, as if they held invitations to his
funeral. Why, I was beginning to shed a few tears myself when
Trimalchio went on, 'Well, as we know we must die, why not live
while we may? I want to see you happy, so let's all take a plunge in
the baths. I'll stake my life you won't regret it. It's as hot as an oven
in there.'

'How right you are,' said Habinnas. 'What I always say is, make
one day last as long as two.'

He rose on his bare feet and followed in Trimalchio's cheerful
footsteps.

I turned to Ascyltus.

'What's your opinion?' I asked. 'Me, I'll pass out on the spot at
the mere sight of a bath.'

'Let's agree to go,' he replied, 'and we'll dodge away in the
crowd as they make for the baths.'

This was a good idea. Giton led us through the colonnade to the
door, where a dog on a chain greeted us with such a row that
Ascyltus fell into a fishpond. I, who had been terrified by a painted
dog, was as drunk as he was, and when I tried to help him from the
water I was dragged into the same abyss. However, we were saved
by a porter who intervened to silence the dog and haul us out
shivering on to dry land. For some time Giton had been retrieving
himself from the dog by a very clever ruse; whenever it barked he
threw it the bits we had saved him from the dinner; diverted by the
food, the beast stilled its rage. But we were freezing, and when we
asked the porter to let us out of the door, he replied, 'You are
mistaken if you think you can go out where you came in. No guest
is ever let out by the same door; you come in one way and you go
out another.'

Wretched creatures! What could we do, imprisoned in a laby- 73
rinth of a novel kind? And now a bath began to be our one desire,
so we asked him of our own accord to lead us to the baths. We
threw off our clothes, which Giton put out to dry in the entrance,
and went in.

The bathhouse was narrow and like a cooling-cistern.
Trimalchio stood upright in it. Even in this position there was no
escape from his intolerable bragging; he said nothing was finer than

to bathe away from the crush, and that the place had once been a corn-mill. In the end he was so tired he had to sit down, and seduced by the acoustics of the room, he opened his drunken mouth wide to the ceiling and began to murder the songs of Menecrates,[58] or so I was told by those who could follow his jargon. The other guests joined hands and pranced round the edge, and set up a deafening noise with their cackles of laughter. Others again, their hands tied behind their backs, tried to lift rings off the tiling with their teeth, or went down on their knees, bent their heads back, and tried to touch the tips of their toes. While they played games, we went to another bath that had been prepared for Trimalchio.

We cleared our drunken heads and were led to a second dining-room, where Fortunata had set out her finery . . . Over the lamps, I noticed little bronze fishermen, entire tables of silver, cups of gilded earthenware all around, and wine filtering through cloth before our eyes. Then Trimalchio said, 'Friends, today one of my slaves celebrates the trimming of his first beard. Touch wood, he's honest and a frugal fellow. So let's wet our throats and feast until daybreak.'

74   As he spoke these words a cock crew. The omen troubled Trimalchio, who ordered wine to be poured under the table and sprinkled in the lamp. And he passed his ring from his left to his right hand, and said, 'There is a reason for the trumpeter's signal. There is a fire somewhere, or someone close whispers goodbye to his soul. Preserve us from such things! Whoever delivers this evil prophet to me shall have his reward.

No sooner had he spoken than a cock was fetched from nearby. Trimalchio gave orders for it to be cooked in a pot. Our exquisite cook, who not long ago had made fishes and birds of a pig, cut the bird to pieces and tossed it into the stewpot. And while Daedalus knocked back a fiery drink, Fortunata ground pepper in a box-wood mill.

When these delicacies were over, Trimalchio looked round at the slaves.

'What, haven't you eaten yet?' he said. 'Off with you, and let some others take your places.'

A new brigade came in, and the old ones shouted, 'Goodbye, Gaius!' and the new ones, 'Hallo Gaius!'

At this point our gaiety was eclipsed for the first time, for among the new waiters was a boy of no mean beauty. Trimalchio fell on him and began a lengthy kiss. So Fortunata, asserting her conjugal rights, heaped abuse on Trimalchio's head, calling him a shit and a scandal for not controlling his passion. She hurled the supreme insult: 'You hound!'

This outcry annoyed Trimalchio and he flung a cup at her head. Fortunata clapped trembling hands to her face and howled as if an eye had been put out. Scintilla was upset too, and took her quivering friend into her arms. An officious slave even applied a cold jar to her cheek, and Fortunata leaned over it groaning and weeping. Trimalchio was defiant.

'Aha!' he cried, 'Doesn't the trollop remember? I took her off the sale-stand, I made her fit for human company. But she puffs up like a frog and won't spit for good luck. She's a clod, not a woman. But if you're born in a hovel you sleep uneasy in a palace. By all that's holy, I'll bring this jackbooted amazon to heel! And just to think that I could have married ten million! What a fool I was! You know I'm not lying. Agatho, the perfumer to the woman next door, took me on one side to say, "I advise you not to let your family die out". But being good-natured as I am, and with no desire to seem capricious, I stuck the axe in my own foot. Well, I'll make you want to dig me up with your own fingernails. And just to let you know here and now what you've brought on yourself: Habinnas, don't put her statue on my tomb, or I shall have no peace even when I'm dead. Just one thing more: to show her I can hurt, I forbid her to kiss me when I'm laid out stiff.'

After this flash of lightning Habinnas implored him to forgo his 75 wrath.

'We all go wrong sometimes. We are men, not gods,' he said.

Scintilla wept and said much the same, and begged him to soften, calling him Gaius and appealing to his true self. Trimalchio was unable to hold back his tears.

'Please, Habinnas,' he said, 'as surely as I hope you enjoy your life-savings, spit in my face if I've done anything wrong. I kissed that most commendable boy, not for his beauty, but because of his virtues. He knows his ten-times table, he can read at sight, he has bought a Thracian rigout from his daily allowance, and he has paid for an armchair and two ladles out of his own money. Doesn't he deserve to be the apple of my eye? But Fortunata is against it! That's how you see it, isn't it, bandy-legs? Take my advice and digest what you have, you kite, and don't make me show my teeth, pretty one, else you'll find out what my temper's like. You know me – once I get something into my head, it sticks there like a ten-inch nail. But to come back to the living. Make yourselves at home, friends. For I was once just as you are now, but I raised myself to this on my own merits. The heart makes the man, and all the rest is rubbish. "I buy well, I sell well," although some people say differently. Happiness! I'm just bursting with it. What, still blubbing, you snuffler? I'll give you what for to whine about! As I was saying, self-help brought me to my fortune. I came out of Asia no bigger than this candlestick. In fact day by day I measured myself by it, and rubbed my lips with the lamp-oil to get a bit of hair on my muzzle all the quicker. All the same, I was my master's cherub for fourteen years. Nothing disgraceful in doing what the master bids. And I did my mistress's pleasure as well. You know what I mean. But hush, hush, I am not one to boast. Finally, as the gods would have it, I turned master in the house, and there I was, his master's brains. The gist of it was that he made me joint-heir with Caesar, and I came into an estate, nobleman's size. Nobody is satisfied with next to nothing. I was burning to do business. To cut a long story short, I built five ships, got a cargo of wine, worth its weight in gold in those days, and sent them to Rome. You would think it was a put-up job; every single ship was wrecked. That's the truth, I'm not making it up. In one day Neptune swooped thirty millions. Was I downhearted? No, I assure you, I felt the loss as if it was nothing. I built some more, bigger and better, more successful, and everybody said I was an intrepid fellow. You know, a big ship has a lot of staying power. Once again I shipped wine, bacon, beans, Capuan perfume, and slaves. This time Fortunata did the right thing; she sold her jewels, her wardrobe, everything, and slipped a hundred gold pieces in my hand. This was the leaven of my pile. There's no delay when the gods are on to something. In one trip I rounded off a good ten million. I promptly bought up all my patron's estates. I built a house, I bought slaves and livestock; whatever I touched grew like a honeycomb. When I was getting more income than the whole country, I threw in my hand. I retired from business and began

moneylending among freedmen. I was completely unwilling to
carry on my affairs, but I was encouraged by an astrologer who
happened to light on our town. He was a little Greek. Name of
Serapa, and well in with the gods. He told me things I had
forgotten, he explained it all from the needle and thread onwards;
he knew what I had in my guts. He might well have told me what
I had for supper the day before. You would have thought he'd
never left my side. You remember, don't you, Habinnas – I think 77
you were on the spot – "You took your wife from a certain place.
You are unlucky in your friends. You never get the gratitude you
deserve. You own vast estates. You nourish a viper in your
bosom," and – though I oughtn't to tell you this – he said I had
thirty years, four months and two days left to live. Moreover I am
soon to come into a legacy. My horoscope says so. And if I can
extend my farms as far as Apulia,[59] I shall have done well enough in
this life. In the meantime, while Mercury watches over me, I have
built this house. You know it was a mere hut – it's a palace now.
Four dining-rooms, twenty bedrooms, two marble colonnades, an
upper storeroom, a bedroom I sleep in myself, a nest for my viper,
a first-rate porter's lodge, and accommodation for all my guests.
Just let me mention that when Scaurus[60] comes here he will go
nowhere else, and his people have a house by the seaside. There
are a great many other things I will show you quite soon. Believe
me, you have a penny, you're worth a penny; have something,
and you will be someone. That's how your friend who was a frog
is now a king. Now, Stichus, bring me the shroud in which I wish
to be buried, and bring the perfumes and a sample from the jar that
shall be poured over my bones.'

Stichus lost no time in fetching a white winding-sheet and a 78
robe into the dining-room. Trimalchio asked us to feel whether
they were made of good wool. He added with a smile, 'Take care,
Stichus, that the mice and moths don't get at them, or I'll burn
you alive. I want to be carried out in style, so that everybody
blesses me.'

Then he opened a pot of spikenard, anointed us all with it, and
said, 'I hope I like it as much when I'm dead as now when I'm
alive.'

He had them pour the wine into a bowl.

'Just make believe you are guests at my funeral,' he said.

The thing was becoming utterly nauseating when Trimalchio, by now far gone in the most bestial drunkenness, ordered in a fresh lot of entertainers – horn-blowers. Propped up by a number of cushions, he stretched himself out to the edge of his couch.

'Pretend I'm dead,' he said.[61] 'Play something nice.'

The horn-blowers sounded a funeral march. The undertaker's man in particular, the most respectable-looking of them all, blew with such force that he roused the entire neighbourhood. Watchmen patrolling the district, under the impression that Trimalchio's house was on fire, suddenly broke down the door and went through the motions with water-buckets, hatchets and considerable uproar.

We seized this most welcome opportunity, gave Agamemnon the slip and fled as fast as we could, as if from a real blaze.

4

Unfaithful lovers and a manic poetaster

We had no torch at hand to help us on our wandering way, nor
did the still of midnight now give us hope of a stranger with a flare.
There was our drunkenness to be considered, and our ignorance
of a neighbourhood that would have baffled us even by day. So for
nearly a whole hour we dragged our bleeding feet over sharp
gravel and shards, until we were saved by Giton's cleverness.
Afraid of missing his way in the daytime, he had been careful
enough to make chalk marks on all the posts and columns. The
lines shone through the thickest night, and their stark whiteness
pointed the way we sought. Yet when we reached our destination
we still had much to sweat over. For the old woman too had spent
the long night swilling drink with her lodgers; you could have set
fire to her without her feeling it, and we might well have stayed
on the doorstep that night if Trimalchio's courier had not turned
up with a convoy of ten carriages. He wasted no time in knocking,
but broke the door of the inn down and let us in through the
breach.

> Ah gods, ah, what a night it was,
> And the bed so soft. In hot embrace
> Through kiss on kiss we poured as one
> Our restless souls.
> Farewell to mortal strife.
> My destruction had begun.

I had no reason to be proud of myself. I was unnerved by the
wine and had let my quivering hands fall to my side, when
Ascyltus, who would contrive every possible outrage, ravished
Giton from me in the dark and brought him to his own bed,

making too free as he wallowed with someone else's boy. Giton
either did not feel the outrage or pretended not to, and in a stolen
embrace Ascyltus fell asleep, oblivious of human rights. When I
awoke I ran a hand all over my bed and found it despoiled of my
delight. Any lover will believe me when I say that I hesitated
whether or not to run them through with my sword and crown
their sleep with death.

Taking the safer course, I shook Giton up with a few blows,
looked fiercely at Ascyltus, and said, 'Since you have wickedly
broken our pact and our mutual friendship, take your things at
once and find some other place to pollute.'

He offered no resistance, yet when we had divided our spoils in
good faith he said, 'And now we must split the boy in two.'

80   I thought it was a parting jest. But he drew his sword with
murderous intent and added, 'You shall not enjoy the booty you
brood over on your own. I need my share, and I will cut it off with
this sword, despised though I am.'

It was my turn to strike the same attitude. I wrapped my cloak
round my arm and took my guard. In the middle of our lunatic
folly the anguished boy grasped our knees, and tearfully begged us
not to make this low inn the scene of a Theban duel,[1] nor to defile
a hallowed and beautiful friendship by spilling one another's blood.

'If you must commit a crime,' he cried, 'here is my bare throat,
turn your hands to that, plunge your blades in it. I am the one who
should die for wiping out your oath of friendship.'

We sheathed our swords after this plea, and Ascyltus was the first
to speak: 'I'm going to put a stop to our quarrel. The boy himself
shall follow whoever he chooses, so at least he will be free to pick
his own brother.'

Persuaded that our long-standing intimacy had passed into a
bond of blood, I had no qualms, and jumped hastily at the proposal.
I put the case to our judge. I had scarcely closed my mouth when,
without any deliberation, without any show of hesitation, he got
up and chose Ascyltus for his brother. I was thunderstruck by this
decision, and collapsed, just as I was, on my bed. I would have
attempted suicide at the verdict if I had not grudged my enemy that
extra triumph. Ascyltus went off gloating over his prize, and left
me, so lately his dearest friend and equal in every fortune, an
outcast in a strange place.

Friendship's a name that clings while it's useful;
The piece comes and goes on the checkered board.
When fate is for us, friends, your smile is wide;
When gone, you show your backs, you basely fly.

A comedy plays: this is the Father,
That the Son; another's named the Rich Man.
But the page turns down on the pleasant parts,
True faces come back, the greasepaint melts away.

But I did not indulge in tears for long. I was afraid Menelaus,[2] the   81
assistant tutor, would add to my troubles by finding me alone at the
inn, so I made a bundle of my things and in sombre mood took a
room at an unfrequented place near the sea.

I shut myself in for three days. My mind was haunted with
loneliness and humiliation. I beat my breast, already weary with
sobbing, I groaned heavily, and broke out again and again with the
same lament: 'Why couldn't the earth open and swallow me
down? Or the sea, so terrible even to the innocent? I fled from
justice, I cheated the arena, I killed my host, and with these titles
to valour I am a beggar, an exile, and lie abandoned in a Greek
town at an inn. And who reduced me to this solitude? An
adolescent infected with every vice, and by his own admission
deserving of exile, who got his freedom by debauch, his birthright
by it, who gambled his young life away, who was treated as a girl
even by those who knew he was a man. And the other one? He
put on a skirt instead of a grown man's wear; his own mother
coaxed him out of his sex; he played a woman's part in the slaves'
quarters; then he couldn't meet his debts, he changed his style of
debauch, forsook the very name of our old friendship, and – the
shame of it – has sold all, like the last prostitute, for one clinging
night. Now the two lovers lie whole nights together in one
embrace, and perhaps they laugh at my solitude when they have
exhausted their lust and themselves. But they won't get away with
it. I am no man, and no freeman, if I do not avenge the insult in
their own guilty blood.'

So saying I buckled on my sword, and with a large meal I got up   82
my strength in case by weakness I defeated my own purpose. I
burst into the street and stalked furiously round the arcades. But
while my face betrayed a savage fury, while I could picture

nothing but blood and slaughter as my hand went again and again
to the hilt of my sword I had dedicated to the task, I was noticed
by a soldier, a deserter in all probability, or some loiterer of the
night.

'Hallo, comrade. What is your regiment, and whose company?'

I lied stoutly about my regiment and my commanding officer.

'But tell me,' he went on, 'do the soldiers of your troop go about
in white shoes?'[3]

My change of face and agitation betrayed a lie, and he ordered
me to lay down my arms and look out for myself.

I had been robbed, and my revenge cut short. I turned back
towards the inn, and as my courage slowly evaporated, I came to be
grateful for the ruffian's audacity.

*   *   *

Unhappy Tantalus![4] Forced on by desire,
He cannot drink though deep in water,
Nor pluck the hanging fruit above.
Let this be the image of a mighty rich man
Who amasses all things but has his fears,
And digests hunger with a dried-up mouth.

*   *   *

It will not altogether do to rely on a plan of action when fate has a
system all her own.

*   *   *

83 I entered a gallery hung with wonderful paintings of every kind. I
saw works from Zeuxis' hand as yet undimmed by the ravages of
time, and I considered, not without a certain thrill of respect,
some *ébauches* by Protogenes, more like reality than Nature herself. Then I came to works by Apelles[5] which the Greeks call
monochromes, and really worshipped them. For the contours of
his figures were rounded off to a lifelikeness with such dexterity
that you would have thought them pictures of their souls as well.
Here, an eagle bore the shepherd-boy of Ida to the heights of
heaven; there, unsullied Hylas refused the wanton Naiad. Apollo
damned his guilty hands and crowned his slackened lyre with a
newborn flower.[6] Among these painted lovers' faces I cried out as

though no one were there, 'So the gods too are touched by love! Jupiter in his heaven found nothing to please him, and went whoring on earth, and yet did no one any harm. The nymph who ravished Hylas would have stayed her passion had she believed Hercules might come to forbid it. Apollo transformed the shade of a boy into a flower, and every tale is of embraces secure from rivalry. But I have taken up with a companion more cruel than Lycurgus himself.'[7]

All at once, as I argued with the breeze, a white-headed old man[8] came into the gallery. His face was emaciated, and seemed to hold promise of some greatness. But his dress was shabby, and it was easy to see from this that he was one of those literary men the rich are prone to despise. He came and stood beside me.

*   *   *

'I am a poet,' he said, 'and not, I hope, of the lowest order of imagination, if the laurels are anything to go by, although favour confers them often enough on worthless heads. "Then why are you so badly dressed?" say you. For that reason: the love of genius never made any man rich.

> Who trusts the hazardous sea, reaps his huge profit;
> Who follows camp and battle may gird himself with gold;
> The cheap flatterer lies drunk on a purple couch;
> The rake earns money by adultery.
> Eloquence alone shivers ragged in winter,
> And helplessly calls on neglected arts.

No doubt about it – if a man is the enemy of every vice and begins 84 to tread the narrow path of righteousness, he at once incurs hatred because of his eccentric ways. For who will approve of conduct unlike his own? What is more, those who only care to accumulate riches would have you believe that nothing is better than what they possess. And they hound out men of letters by whatever means they can, to show that they too are amenable to money.'

*   *   *

'I don't know why, but poverty is sister to good sense.'[9]

*   *   *

'I wish the man who hates my honesty were innocent enough for me to appease him. But he's a hardened thief and sharper than the pimps themselves.'[10]

*   *   *

85   'When I went to Asia in the suite of a Treasury official, I stayed in Pergamum.[11] I was glad to live there, not only for the stylish quarters, but also because my host had a very handsome son. I thought out a scheme for becoming his lover without being suspected by his father. As often as mention was made at table of the abuse of such attractive boys, I got so violently heated, so extremely chagrined at having my ears assailed by such obscene talk, that his mother, more than anyone, took me to be one of the moral philosophers. So I now escorted the boy to his lecture-rooms, I arranged his studies, I taught and tutored, I took care to see that no one who might seduce him set foot in the house.

One holiday, when lessons were curtailed, we were lazing on a couch, too indolent to retire to our room after a long day's enjoyment. About midnight I realised that my boy was wide awake. I whispered a fearful prayer.

"Dear Venus," I said, "if I may kiss this boy without his noticing, tomorrow I will give him a pair of turtledoves."

As soon as he heard the price of my desires he began to snore. Getting close I was able to steal a few kisses. Satisfied with this beginning, I was up early in the morning to bring the pair of doves he awaited. So I discharged my vow.

86   The following night the same thing was allowed, and I raised my stake.

"If," I said, "I may caress him sensuously without his feeling it, I will award him two cocks, the most gallant of the yard, for obliging me."

At this promise the boy moved up of his own accord, and I think he was afraid I might fall asleep. I soon calmed his anxiety, and indulged in his body, saving the supreme pleasure. When day came I made the boy happy with what I had promised him.

The third night I again had as much liberty, and I gained the sham sleeper's ear.

"Immortal gods," I said, "if I may take the full pleasure I desire from this sleeping child, for that I will give him tomorrow a

Macedonian racehorse, one of the best, on condition that he feels nothing."

The boy never fell into a deeper sleep than now. First I touched his milk-white breast, then my lips closed on his and I crowned all my desires in one.

The next morning he sat in his bedroom, expecting the usual thing to happen. But you know how much easier it is to buy doves and cocks than a horse, and anyway I was afraid so sizeable a gift might make my generosity suspect. I strode around for some hours, returned to my lodgings, and did no more than kiss the boy. He looked about, and throwing his arms round my neck, "Sir," he said, "where is my horse?"

Although the offence excluded me from the *entrée* I had gained, 87 I was to win my privilege once more. A few days went by, and a similar chance threw us into the same good fortune. As soon as I heard his father snore, I started asking the boy to make his peace with me, that is to say, to suffer my pleasure. I used all the arguments that lust dictates. Utterly enraged, his only reply was, "Go to sleep, or I'll call my father."

Nothing is so difficult that it cannot be brought about by a dirty trick or two. While he repeated, "I'll wake my father," I insinuated myself and took my pleasure, in spite of poorly-disguised resistance. But my attack did not seem to displease him, and after a lengthy complaint that my deception had earned him the ridicule of his schoolfellows, to whom he had boasted of my largesse, he said, "You will see I am not like you. Start again, if you want to."

So we forgot our differences, I obtained my pardon, and fell asleep after profiting by his good humour. But this second caress was not enough for a youth in the full flower of an age that welcomed such delights. He woke me from my sleep with the words, "What, no more?"

It had not yet actually become tiresome, so breathing heavily and sweating, I did my best to please him, and dropped back to sleep with fatigue. Less than an hour later, he was pinching me: "Why aren't we doing it?"

Then I, after being woken up so often, got into a thoroughly bad temper, and to turn the tables on him said, "Go to sleep, or *I'll* call your father." '

*   *   *

88 I was encouraged by this tale, and asked the old man, more
experienced than I was, about the antiquity of the pictures, and
what the point was in some that were unintelligible to me, what
caused the apathy of the present age, why we lost the fine arts, of
which painting, among others, had left no trace whatsoever.

'Lust for money,' he replied, 'was at the root of this change. In
the old days virtue unadorned was sufficient, the liberal arts
flourished, and the height of rivalry among men was to ensure that
nothing of benefit to posterity should remain undiscovered. In this
spirit Democritus[12] distilled the juices out of all known herbs, and
spent his life in experiments to discover the forces hidden in stones
and plants. Eudoxus grew old on the peak of the highest mountain
in order to unravel the motions of the stars and heavens, and three
times Chrysippus purged his brain with hellebore to restore his
inventive powers. To come back to the plastic arts, Lysippus was so
engrossed with the perfection of one statue that he died of self-
neglect, and Myron, who all but put the soul of man and beast into
bronze and iron, left himself no heir. But we founder in wine and
wenches, and can't even face up to the arts we have with us; we
blame the past, we learn of nothing but vice, and teach it too.
Where's our dialectic? Where's astronomy? And the royal road to
wisdom? Who has ever entered a temple to pray that he might
attain eloquence? Or tap the springhead of philosophy? They don't
even ask for health in mind or body, but the very moment they are
on the doors of the Capitol, this man promises a gift if he can bury
a rich relation, that one if he can root out a hidden treasure, and
another if he can come into an easy thirty million. The Senate
itself, that sets the standard of what is right and proper, habitually
promises the Capitol a thousand pounds of gold, and to put an end
to any doubts about greed, tries to influence Jupiter himself with
money. So don't be surprised that painting is decadent when gods
and men alike see more beauty in a nugget of gold than in anything
89 Apelles and Phidias ever did, the poor eccentric Greeks! But I see
you are fascinated by the picture representing the Sack of Troy. I
will try to explain the work in verse:

> Now the tenth harvest of the Trojan siege[13]
> Saw their state critical and wrought with fear;
> In Calchas the prophet faith hovered nigh

Black doubt. Apollo spoke, and Ida's peaks
Were shorn of wood. The oaks fell in one heap
To make the image of a valiant horse.
A vast hollow opened, a secret cave
To hide a host. The valour of ten years'
Angry war was crowded in, and stern Greeks
Lay waiting thick in their votive offering.
O my country, we thought a thousand ships
Were beaten off, the land redeemed from war:
This was the legend engraved on the beast,
This the lie Sinon framed and asserted,
The lie that led us down to our doom.
The mob was free; released from war they rushed
From the gates to pray. Their cheeks streamed with tears,
Those tears of joy well known to anguished hearts.
But fear soon dried them, for Laocoon,
The wild-haired priest of Neptune, inspired
The shouting crowd. First he drew back his spear
And stabbed the horse's belly, but his hand
Was stayed by fate, the shaft recoiled; it gave
The whole fraud an air of veracity.
A second time he steeled his weakened hand
And sheered his axe through the thick-ribbed flank.
The men inside their prison shook, their moan
Lent the massive oak a strange and fearful sigh.
The captive band went forth to capture Troy,
And changed the face of war by new deceits.
But more prodigious signs now followed on:
Where lofty Tenedos crowds out the sea
With its huge back, the billows seethed and swelled,
The breaker leaped back to furrow the calm,
And sounded like the distant noise of oars
In the silent night, when ships ride the sea,
And the surface groans under moving keels.
We looked again: two twin-coiling serpents
Sweep tide-borne to the rocks; with swollen breasts
Like lofty ships they drive the foam aside.
Their tails resound, their waving crests accord
With the fire of their eyes; a thunderbolt

Burns brilliant on the waters, that tremble
At their hiss. Our hearts were horror-stricken.
There stood the two sons of Laocoon
In Phrygian wear with sacred ornaments,
Pledged to sacrifice, when suddenly
The serpents entwined their shimmering lengths
Around. Their tiny hands flew to their faces,
Each thought of his brother, not of himself;
Love changed the roles, by mutual fear alone
Death took the two unhappy sons. Behold
The father, too weak to help, join his own
In death. Already gorged with two bodies
The serpents attack the man by his limbs.
They drag him down. The victim priest lies there
Among the altars, and beats on the earth.
Thus they profane most holy things, and Troy,
The city near to doom, first lost her gods.
Now Phoebe at the full spread her white beam
To lead the outer stars with radiant light,
When the Greeks unlatched the cavernous horse
And poured their heroes on Priam's sons,
All drowned in the night or dulled in their wine.
Like the Thessalian steed loosed from his yoke
As he starts head high, shaking a long mane,
The leaders try their armoured strength, draw swords,
Brandish shields, and do battle. This hews down
Enemies heavy with wine, lengthening
Their sleep to utter death. Here, another
Lights his torches at their very altars,
And calls the gods of Troy upon the Trojans.'

90   At this point in Eumolpus' recital some of the people walking in
the colonnade flung stones at him. Familiar with this reception of
his genius, he covered his head and fled from the temple. I was
rather afraid he would earn me the name of poet, too. So following
in the wake of his flight, I reached the seashore.

Once out of range of their missiles, when we could rest, 'Tell
me,' I said, 'where do you hope to get with this affliction of yours?
You've been hanging about me under two hours, yet you've more

often spoken poetically than like a human being. No wonder people chase you with stones. I'll fill my pockets with stones too, and every time you're beside yourself, I'll bleed your head for it.'

His face changed. 'My boy,' he said, 'I wasn't born yesterday. Indeed, whenever I go into a theatre to recite something I get this kind of welcome from the crowd. So to remove this bone of contention with you, I shall abstain the whole day from this food of the gods.'

'What's more,' I said, 'if you will swear off this folly for the day, we can have supper together.'

* * *

I charged the keeper of my little place with preparing a modest meal.

* * *

I saw Giton standing against the wall with towels and scrapers, sad 91 and perturbed. Clearly an unwilling servant. And to confirm what I saw . . . He turned me a face softened with joy, and said, 'Pity me, brother. I can open my heart only where there are no weapons. Take me from this bloody robber, and punish your repentant judge with whatever brutalities you like. To die by your wish would be a great relief in my misery.'

I made him stop his pleading in case our plans were discovered. I left Eumolpus reciting poetry in the bath, dragged Giton through a dim, filthy side-entrance, and flew with him to my own rooms.

When the door was shut I threw my arms round him and crushed my lips on his tear-stained face. For a long time neither of us spoke. The boy's lovely body shook with endless sobbing.

'Oh, unworthy weakness,' I cried. 'I love you although you left me. And where a gaping wound was in my heart, no scar can be found. What have you to say, you who yielded to an outsider's love? Did I deserve that injury?'

Feeling himself still loved, his features relaxed.

* * *

'I referred our love to no other judge. But I will say no more, I will blot it from my mind, if you repent sincerely.' Tears and groans went with my flood of words.

He wiped his face with his cloak, and said, 'Encolpius, please, I appeal to your honest memory; did I leave you, or did you betray me? For my part, I admit it quite openly; when I saw two armed men, I sided with the stronger.'

I threw my arms round his neck, gave this wise heart a long kiss, and held him close to me to show we were reconciled and that our friendship lived once more in the deepest sincerity.

92   It was now quite dark. The woman had seen to my order for supper, when Eumolpus knocked at the door.

'How many are you?' I asked, in the meantime spying eagerly through a crack in the door to see if Ascyltus had come with him. He was my only visitor, and I opened up at once. He dropped on my bed, and when he caught sight of Giton waiting at table before his very eyes, he nodded, 'Good for Ganymede![14] Everything will go well for us today.'

I was not pleased with this brash overture, and I was afraid I had let another Ascyltus into my rooms. Eumolpus returned to the charge, and when the boy offered him a drink he said, 'I like you more than the whole bathful.'

He drained the cup dry in one gulp and said he had never tasted anything more acid.

'And would you believe it,' he went on, 'I was nearly beaten up while I was in the water, simply for trying to recite poetry to the people sitting round the edge, and after I was thrown out of the baths just as I was out of the theatre, I looked for you in every corner and shouted for Encolpius. Down the other end was a young man with nothing on – he had lost his clothes – and he kept indignantly calling for Giton, and made just as much noise about it. I was taken for a madman by the boys. They derided me with the most insolent imitations, but *he* gathered a huge crowd round him, and they applauded *him* and were extremely respectful in their admiration. For his member was so prodigious that the man himself was to be mistaken for a tassel on it. What a worker! I can imagine him starting one day and finishing the next. And he was snapped up at once; somebody or other, a Roman knight, a rake, so they said, put his cloak round his shoulders as he wandered about and led him home, no doubt to ensure sole title to this great good fortune. As for me, I might never have got my clothes back from the attendant if I had not produced somebody to vouch for me. So much the more advantageous it is to brush up your wick than your wit.'

While Eumolpus was telling this I kept changing my expression, glad when my enemy was in a bad way, sorry when it went well with him. However, I was silent, and set out the bill of fare as if the tale meant nothing to me.

* * *

'They despise whatever is lawful, and their hearts, grown lethargic 93 through uncertain tastes, long for things forbidden, and nothing else.'[15]

> The pheasant won from Colchis
> And African guinea-fowls
> Taste good because these birds are rare,
> While the plain white goose and the duck
> With speckled bright feathers
> Have merely an ordinary savour.
> Parrot-fish drawn from distant shores,
> A catch from the Syrtes costing a shipwreck,
> Are all the rage; we're tired of mullet now.
> The mistress excels the wife,
> Cinnamon puts the rose to blush.
> The very far-fetched will pass for the best.

'I thought you promised,' I said, 'not to compose any verse today? Really, you might have spared us that at least; we haven't stoned you. If any of the men drinking under this roof smells the name of poet, he will rouse the whole neighbourhood and do us all in for one and the same reason. For pity's sake, don't forget the art gallery or the baths.'

For saying this I was rebuked by Giton, a gentle soul, and he said I was wrong to abuse my elders; I forgot my duties as a host, by my impoliteness I was spoiling the meal I had been kind enough to arrange for him. He gave me a great deal more advice both tolerant and shy that went well with his personal beauty.

* * *

'How very fortunate your mother was,' said Eumolpus, 'to give 94 birth to a child like you. Be good and do well! How rare it is to see wisdom and beauty combined! And don't think you have been wasting your breath. You have found a lover! I will fill my poems with your praises. As your protector and teacher, I shall follow you everywhere, even without your permission. There's no harm done to Encolpius; he has another love.'

It was a good thing for Eumolpus that the soldier had taken my sword away, otherwise I would have wreaked the anger I had worked up against Ascyltus in the poet's blood. Giton did not fail to notice this. He left the room, supposedly to fetch water.

This discreet departure put an end to my wrath, and as my fury cooled off a little, I said, 'Eumolpus, I would rather have you recite, even that, than have you harbour such desires. I am a violent man, and you are a lecher. You can see that our characters don't fit together. Imagine you have to deal with a lunatic; give way to my madness; in other words, clear out, and quick too.'

Eumolpus was dumbfounded by this threat. He asked no reason for my anger, but went straight out of the room, slammed the door to and locked it, the thing I least expected. He snatched the key out and ran looking for Giton.

I was a prisoner. I resolved to hang myself and put an end to it all. I had already tied my belt to the frame of the bed, which was up against the wall, and was putting my head in the noose, when the door was undone, and in came Eumolpus with Giton to recall me from the very brink of death to the light of life. Giton in particular, whose grief now rose to a savage fury, uttered a cry, pushed me with his two hands, and forced me on to the bed.

'You're wrong, Encolpius,' he said, 'if you think you can bring about your own death before I die. I thought of it first. I was looking for a sword at Ascyltus' place. If I hadn't found you I would have jumped over a precipice. And just to show that death is never far from those who seek it, watch for yourself what you wanted me to see.'

With these words he seized a razor from Eumolpus' valet, slashed at his throat once, twice, and collapsed in a heap at our feet. I gave a shriek of horror, fell as he had done, and sought the road to death with the same steel blade.

But there was not the slightest trace of a wound on Giton, and I felt no pain at all. The razor had no cutting edge. It was purposely blunted, to give apprentices the confidence of a fully-fledged barber, and had acquired a kind of coating round it. This was why the valet let the blade be taken without turning a hair, and why Eumolpus had not interfered in our farcical suicide.

While this lovers' interlude was being played, the landlord came 95 in with the rest of our scant dinner. He took one look at us sprawling disgracefully on the floor and said, 'You there, are you drunk? Or runaway slaves? Or both? Who turned that bed up? What's the meaning of all these furtive goings-on? Blast it, I know; you weren't going to pay the rent of your room, you were going to flee into the open night. But no such luck. I'll have you know the rooms don't belong to some poor old widow, but to Marcus Mannicius.'

'What,' roared Eumolpus, 'threatening us too?' And at the same time he struck him in the face with all his might.

However, the man pitched an earthenware pot, empty now so many guests had been served, at Eumolpus' head. He heard him cry as it split his forehead open, and fled from the room. Eumolpus was furious at this insult. He grasped a wooden candlestick, followed him as he made off, and avenged his bloody brow in a hail of blows. The servants came running up, and a whole crowd of besotted lodgers. I now had a chance of getting even with Eumolpus, so I shut him out, and treated the churl as he treated me. I was left without a rival, and had the room to myself for the rest of the night.

In the meantime cooks and lodgers were manhandling him now he was outside. One stuck a spit of spluttering-hot tripe in his eyes, while another took a prong from the meat-safe and stood in fighting pose. To crown it all, a gummy-eyed old woman, in a linen cloth creeping with filth, and shuffling on uneven clogs, dragged on an enormous dog by a chain and set him at Eumolpus. But he was keeping all comers at bay with his candlestick.

We saw everything through a hole in the door, made not long 96 before when the handle was wrenched off, and I cheered them on as Eumolpus got a drubbing. Giton, with his usual compassion, was all for opening the door and helping the man in his peril. But with my resentment still burning, I did not stay my hand, but fetched the kind-hearted child a sharp blow on the head with my clenched fist. He sat down on the bed to cry. Meanwhile, putting now one eye and now another to the hole, I feasted on Eumolpus' unhappy lot as on a good meal, and recommended him to call for help.

Then the manager of the lodging-house, Bargates, was disturbed at his dinner, and his two porters carried him – he suffered from gout – right into the thick of the brawl. After raving interminably at drunkards and runaway slaves in a raucous and ill-tempered voice, he turned to stare at Eumolpus, and said, 'Oh you elegant, elegant poet, so it was you, was it? And these filthy slaves haven't gone any the quicker? They dared lay hands on you?'

*   *   *

'My mistress cold-shoulders me. Do me a favour, slang her in some verses, so that she is ashamed.'

*   *   *

97   While Eumolpus was exchanging a few private words with Bargates, a crier came into the place with a constable and quite a few others. Waving a torch that spread more smoke than light, he made this announcement: 'Lost recently in the public baths; one boy, aged about sixteen, curly-headed, effeminate, attractive, answers to the name of Giton. One thousand pieces reward on return or for information as to his whereabouts.'

Not far from the crier stood Ascyltus wrapped in a multi-coloured cloak, displaying particulars and the promised sum on a silver plate. I ordered Giton under the bed at once, and told him to hook his feet and hands on the webbing of the frame that supported the mattress, and to stretch under the bed to escape inquisitive hands, just as Ulysses of old clung to the belly of a ram.[16] Giton did not have to be told twice. In an instant he had slipped his hands in and was clamped up. He had beaten Ulysses at his own game. To leave no room for suspicion, I filled out the bed with my own clothes, and moulded the shape of a single man of my size with them.

Meanwhile, Ascyltus, who had gone round all the rooms with the summoner, arrived at mine, and his hopes rose when he found the door elaborately bolted. The constable put his hatchet between the joints and loosened the bolt. I fell at Ascyltus' feet and implored him, in memory of our friendship and the misfortunes we had shared, at least to let me see Giton. To add colour to my hypo-critical prayers, I went on, 'I know, Ascyltus, I know you have come to kill me. Else why bring these axes? Then glut your anger.

Here, I offer you my neck, shed the blood you are really after while you pretend to search.'

Ascyltus denied any malicious intention. He assured me he was only looking for his deserter; he had never willed the death of any man or suppliant, still less of a friend he held most dear even after their fatal quarrel.

But the constable was no idler. He took a cane from the innkeeper and pushed it under the bed, and poked it in everything, even the holes in the walls. Giton shrank from the thrusts, drew in his breath most gently, and held a *tête-à-tête* with the bedbugs. The room's broken door could keep nobody out. In rushed Eumolpus with an anguished expression. 98

'The thousand is mine,' he cried, 'I'm going after the crier to tell him Giton is in your hands, as your treachery fully deserves.'

I fell and hugged his knees, but he was unmoved. I begged him not to kill the dying, and added, 'Your outburst would be justified if you could surrender your quarry. But he has escaped into the crowd, and I've no idea where he's gone. For pity's sake, Eumolpus, fetch the boy back, even if you have to give him to Ascyltus.'

Just as I was winning him round to my line of thought, Giton, so full of breath he was unable to hold it a moment longer, sneezed three times in rapid succession. The bed shook. Eumolpus spun round at the noise: 'Bless you, Giton!'

He raised the mattress and saw our Ulysses, whom even a ravenous Cyclops might have spared. Then he turned on me, and said, 'Well, you thief, you daren't tell the truth even when caught red-handed. And if the god who intervenes in mortal affairs hadn't wrested a sign from the boy as he hung there, I should have been wandering round the pot-houses looking like a fool.'

*   *   *

Giton was far more ingratiating than I. He began by staunching the wound in Eumolpus' forehead with cobwebs soaked in oil. Next he exchanged his small coat for the poet's torn clothes, and seeing him a little mollified, put his arms round him and smothered him with a poultice of kisses. Then he said, 'Our fate, dear father, is in your hands, yours alone. If you love your Giton, the first thing is to save him. If only fierce flames would devour me, or the icy sea engulf me! I am the object, the cause of all these crimes. If I died, it might bring two friends together who have quarrelled.'

*　　*　　*

99 'Always and everywhere,[17] I have lived by enjoying each day as if it were the last and its light should never return.'

*　　*　　*

My face streaming with tears, I begged and prayed him to be friends with me again. I said it was not in the power of lovers to control their raging jealousy. I would try never to do or say anything more that could offend him. Only, as a highly-cultured man, he should remove all vexation from his mind, leaving no scar behind: 'The snow lies long on rough and uncultivated ground, but where the land turns bright under the master-plough, the light hoarfrost vanishes while you are speaking. So anger settles in our hearts; on rough hearts it lies long, on cultivated it soon melts.'

'Just to prove to you the truth of what you say,' said Eumolpus, 'with this kiss my anger expires. There, and may everything turn out for the best! Get your packs ready and follow me, or lead the way if you'd rather.'

He was still talking when the door was noisily pushed open, and there on the step stood a sailor with a shaggy beard, and he said, 'You're late, Eumolpus. As if you didn't know there was any hurry.'

We all rose at once and Eumolpus woke his man, who had been asleep for some time, and ordered him to bring out his baggage. With Giton's help I stuffed all we had into a sack, murmured a prayer to the stars, and boarded the ship.[18]

5

The adventures on Lichas' ship and on the way to Croton

'It is tiresome that the boy should so please a stranger. But after all, aren't the best things in life common property? The sun shines on everyone. The moon and her unnumbered host of stars guide the very beasts to their pasture. Is there anything more beautiful than water? Yet it flows for all. Is love alone, then, to be more a furtive act than a bounty? No, I will have no goods at all unless the world at large sighs for them. One man, and old at that, is no serious rival. If he wants to take a liberty his short breath will be against him.'

I made these points with no great confidence, deceiving myself against my better judgement. Then I wrapped my head in my cloak and pretended to sleep. Suddenly, as if fate had conspired to shatter my calm of mind, I heard a voice from the deck say with a groan, just like this: 'So he played me for a fool, did he?'

It was a man's voice, and one vaguely familiar to my ear. My heart beat fast with the shock. Then it was a woman, equally indignant, exploding with greater violence: 'If some god would just deliver that Giton into my hands, I'd have a first-class reception ready for him, the shirker!'

We were both stunned by what we heard, sounds so unexpected that they froze the blood in our veins. For me especially it was as though I were hounded in some confused nightmare, and for some time I could not utter a word. With trembling hands I clutched at Eumolpus' clothes as he was dozing off and said, 'Honestly, father, whose ship is this, who's aboard? Can you tell me?'

He was testy through being disturbed: 'So this is why you chose an out-of-the-way spot on deck to settle in, to prevent our getting any sleep! What can it possibly matter to you to know that Lichas of Tarentum is master of this ship, carrying Tryphaena to exile[1] in that city?'

101   I shuddered at this thunderbolt. I bared my throat and cried, 'Fate, at last it's all up! You have won!'

Giton had fainted some time ago and had fallen across me. A profuse sweating brought us both to our senses, and then I caught Eumolpus by the knee: 'Pity on us! We are dead men. In the name of our common studies, help us! Our time has come. Death, unless you prevent it, may be a mercy.'

Staggered by this menacing outburst, Eumolpus swore by all the gods that he knew nothing of our plight, he was not guilty of the sinister design I imputed, but had taken us aboard as companions with an open mind and in all good faith, and he had reserved his own passage long ago.

'And what are these traps?' he wanted to know. 'What new Hannibal[2] is sailing with us? Lichas of Tarentum is a very worthy man and is not only ship's master, and owner, but he has a number of estates and a commercial company. He is carrying a special export cargo. That is your Cyclops, your pirate-king, to whom we are indebted for this voyage. And then there is Tryphaena, the most beautiful woman in the world, who goes hither and thither for pleasure's sake.'

'Precisely the ones,' breathed Giton, 'we are escaping from.'

In a few swift words he explained their hatred and our present danger to a quaking Eumolpus. He was bewildered, and no help at all. He asked us each to suggest something.

'Imagine,' he said, 'we are in the Cyclops' den. We have to find a way out, unless we stage a shipwreck and get out of peril like that.'

'No,' said Giton, 'persuade the pilot, with money, of course, to call in at a harbour. Insist that your brother cannot stand the sea and is on his last legs. You can colour your hoax with a tortured look and some tears; the pilot will be moved to compassion and will be on your side.'

'Impossible,' said Eumolpus. 'A ship of this size,' he explained, 'can only put in to landlocked harbours, and your brother's sudden collapse is improbable. And remember, Lichas may wish to visit the sick out of politeness. You can see what a favour we would be doing ourselves by fetching down the master when we want to escape him. But suppose the ship could deviate from her distant course, suppose Lichas didn't do the sick-bed rounds; how could we disembark without being seen by all and sundry? Cover our heads? Leave them

bare? Cover them, and everyone will offer his arm to the sick![3] Bare,
it would be no less than calling attention to ourselves.'

'Wouldn't it be better,' I said, 'to fall back on something daring? 102
Slide down a rope into the cock-boat, cut the painter, and leave
the rest to fate? Not that I am inviting Eumolpus to share this risk;
what right have we to burden the innocent with troubles not his
own? All I ask is for chance to help us down.'

'Quite a good plan if you can get it going,' said Eumolpus. 'But
everyone will see you leave, especially the pilot, who is on watch
the whole night through and even has an eye on the motions of the
stars. And however much you might cheat his unsleeping vigilance,
and you were trying to escape from another part of the ship, as
things are it is precisely by the stern, by the helm itself, that you
would want to slide down, because the rope that keeps the cock-
boat is paid out from these quarters. What is more, Encolpius, I am
surprised it did not occur to you that one sailor is always posted on
duty in the boat day and night, and you could only dispose of this
sentry by killing him or throwing him overboard by main force.
Question your own bravado as to whether you could do that. As for
my coming with you, I will face any danger that offers us a chance
of safety. For I suppose even you do not wish to abandon your lives,
like things of no worth, for no reason at all. See whether you can
agree to this. I roll you up into two hold-alls, strap you round, and
place you among my baggage as clothes, leaving a few holes, of
course, through which you can take in air and food. Then I raise the
cry that two of my slaves have thrown themselves in the sea during
the night for fear of greater punishment. Once we are in port, I
disembark you as so much baggage without arousing any suspicion.'

'Oh really,' I said, 'tie us up like solid bodies, whose bowels
never bark their alarm, or like beings who never sneeze or snore?
Just because the trick came off once on a notorious occasion?[4]
What if a calm, or bad weather, kept us there longer than that?
What should we do? Even clothes that are parcelled up too long
wear through at the creases, and papers tied in bundles lose their
shape. We are young, we are not used to work; must we suffer
being baled in cloth and lashed like statues?'

*   *   *

'We must find another means of escape. Think over my inspiration.

As a literary man, Eumolpus must carry ink. We use this to black ourselves out from head to foot. Then we shall be at your beck and call as Ethiopian slaves, without having to put up with such torture. The new colour will deceive our enemies.'

'Oh yes, why not?' said Giton. 'And please circumcise us so we look like Jews, and bore holes in our ears like the Arabs, and chalk our faces so that Gaul claims us as hers. As if colour by itself could change the features and it was unnecessary for everything to be one consistent whole to maintain the deception! Imagine the dye staining our faces for some length of time, and suppose no drop of water ever spots our skin, and the ink doesn't stick to our clothes, as it so often does even without adding gum; tell me then, can we bloat our lips into those repulsive folds? Or crinkle our hair with the iron? Sear our foreheads with scars? Bend our legs until they're bandy? Turn our feet in and hobble on our ankles? Trim our beards to an exotic cut? Artificial dye stains the body, but doesn't change it. Listen to my desperate idea: muffle our heads in what we wear and plunge into the deep.'

103 'The gods and all mankind forbid,' cried Eumolpus, 'that you should end your life in so abject a manner. Better do what I say. As you know from the affair of the razor, my man is also a barber. He will shave both your heads on the spot, eyebrows as well. Then I will carefully mark your foreheads with an inscription so that you appear to have been punished by branding. These letters will both avert the suspicions of your pursuers and conceal your faces beneath the marks of punishment.'

We put the ruse into operation at once. We made cautiously for the side of the boat and submitted our heads and eyebrows to the barber for a shave. Eumolpus covered our brows with enormous letters, and generously marked our faces all over with characters to show we were runaway slaves.

It so happened that one of the passengers, leaning over the side of the ship to relieve his queasy stomach, noticed by the light of the moon a barber, hard at work at an unpropitious hour. He cursed this for an omen, as it seemed to be the last ritual of shipwrecked men, and buried himself in his bunk. With all our feigned deafness to the curse of the vomiting man, we fell into a melancholy mood, and spent the last hours of the night in cautious silence or in fitful sleep.

* * *

'I thought I heard[5] Priapus[6] say in a dream, "You are looking for   104
Encolpius. Let me tell you that I have led him aboard your ship." '

Tryphaena shuddered and said, 'Anyone would think we had
slept together, for I dreamed that the statue of Neptune I noticed in
a temple at Baiae appeared and said, "You will find Giton on
Lichas' ship." '

'All of which goes to show,' said Eumolpus, 'that Epicurus[7] was
an admirable man. He condemns humbugs of this kind in a very
witty fashion.'

But Lichas first exorcised any possible harm resulting from
Tryphaena's dream and then said, 'What is there to stop us
searching the ship to show we aren't abjuring divine providence
out of hand?'

The man who had surprised us at our pathetic shifts the night
before – his name was Hesus – suddenly exclaimed, 'Then who are
these people who were shaving last night by moonlight? An
awfully bad example, I must say. I've always heard no mortal being
is allowed to cut his hair or nails on board except when the winds
and the waves are at odds.'

At this Lichas went white with rage and fear.   105

'So,' he said, 'they've been cutting hair on shipboard, and in the
dead of night too? Fetch the offenders. Quick! I must know whose
heads are to fall in order to purify my ship.'

'It is I who am responsible,' said Eumolpus. 'I did it for luck,
having to be aboard the same ship. As these rogues had long shaggy
hair I didn't want to seem to use the ship as a prison-hole, and I
ordered the dirty scoundrels to be cleaned up. And at the same
time, well, I thought the letters that mark them wouldn't be
obscured by their hair, and they would be fully visible for all to
read. Among other things, they squandered my money on a
woman, one between two, and I hauled them out the night before
dripping with wine and ointment. The fact is, they still reek of the
relics of my inheritance.'

*   *   *

So it was decided that each of us should have forty stripes inflicted
on him to appease the patron god of the ship. Nor did they brook
any delay. Sailors with rope-ends fell upon us in a fury and tried to
propitiate their guardian with our ineffectual blood. For my part, I

stood up to three lashes with Spartan composure.[8] But Giton let
out such a yell at the first blow that the well-known sound of his
voice penetrated to Tryphaena's ear. She was not the only one
moved to pity. All her servants were drawn by the familiar tones
and raced up to him as he was being flogged. But Giton's exceptional beauty had already disarmed the sailors and entreated these
bullies better than any words, when the maids screamed out
together, 'It's Giton! Giton! Oh, do stop, you brutes! Oh, madame, help! It's Giton!'

Tryphaena was already convinced, and as her ear caught this cry
she flew to the boy's side. Lichas, who knew me only too well, ran
up as though he had heard my voice, and without glancing at my
hands or my face, at once looked down and grasped my member,
with the words, 'How do you do, Encolpius?'

Small wonder that Ulysses' nurse,[9] twenty years on, recognised
the scar that betrayed his identity twenty years later, when this
clever man so shrewdly put his finger on a runaway slave's one
decisive feature, in spite of my disguising every part of my face and
body. Tryphaena was in tears. She had been taken in by our faked
punishment, thinking the brands on our foreheads were really the
marks of prisoners, and in a hushed voice she asked us what jail had
delayed our wanderings, and whose hands had been so cruel as to
inflict such a sentence. But perhaps some such harsh treatment was
only the expected reward of runaway slaves who had come to
despise their own good . . .

106   Lichas was hopping mad with rage: 'Oh, you simpleton of a
woman! As if these wounds and letters came from a branding-iron!
Would to God their foreheads had really been defaced with this
scribble; it would have afforded us some satisfaction at least. But we
have been imposed on by the antics of an actor and have been
fooled by forged inscriptions.'

Tryphaena had not abandoned all hope of carnal pleasure, and
was disposed to pity, but then Lichas had not forgotten the
seduction of his wife[10] and the insult offered him in Hercules'
Walk.

His face convulsed with increasing anger, he cried, 'The immortal gods have a hand in the affairs of mortal men, as no doubt you
are aware, Tryphaena. They led these criminals to board my ship
unawares, and let us know they had done it by dreams that

coincided. Now consider if we could possibly pardon them when a god himself has delivered them to us to punish. Personally, I am not vindictive, but I have an uneasy feeling we shall suffer in return if I let them off.'

Tryphaena was swayed by this superstitious talk, and denied being opposed to punishment. On the contrary, she approved of the complete justice of this reprisal. Had she not been as heavily wronged as Lichas,[11] had not her reputation for modesty been flouted in public?

*   *   *

'I believe they have chosen me[12] for this task because I am a man of some standing, and they have asked me to reconcile them with their former friends. You do not really think our young men were driven into such a trap by chance alone, when the first precaution of every traveller is to find out into whose care he commits himself. Ease your mind; it has already been calmed by retribution; let the men proceed freely and fairly to their destination. Even a barbarous and unforgiving master checks his cruelty when repentance brings back the runaway slave; we are lenient to the enemy who surrenders. What more can you want? What more do you wish for? The youths lie prostrate before your very eyes; they are of free birth and honest, and more than either of these things, they were once bound to you by ties of intimacy. I swear that if they had embezzled your money or hurt you by betraying your trust, you might well be satisfied by the punishment you have just seen. Look, slavery is written on their brows; these freeborn heads have voluntarily incurred a punishment that outlaws them.'

Lichas interrupted this plea for mercy: 'Don't confuse the issue, but treat each point as it arises. First of all, if they came of their own accord, why were their heads stripped of hair? Disguising yourself means you want to deceive, not to make amends. And then, if they wanted to fight for their pardon through a spokesman, why did you do all you could to conceal your protégés? All of which goes to show that accident alone drove the defaulters into the trap, and that you searched for some means to avoid the onset of our displeasure. As for trying to slander us by using such terms as 'honest' and 'of free birth', take care not to ruin your case by overconfidence. What should the victim do when the guilty run headlong into the noose? But they were our friends! Then they deserve to be dealt with all the more severely, for who harms a stranger will be known as a ruffian, but the man who injures his friends is nothing less than a parricide.'

Eumolpus countered this damning argument: 'I am aware that nothing tells against these unhappy young men so much as their getting rid of their hair by night. From which you conclude that they chanced on the ship and did not choose it. I should like you to accept my explanation as frankly as the act itself was innocent. Before they embarked, they wished to ease their heads of an irksome and futile weight, but the wind got up suddenly and they had to postpone their toilet. They never supposed it mattered where they started what they wanted to do, being ignorant of omens and usage at sea.'

'But why did they have to shave themselves to petition me?' persisted Lichas. 'Unless a bald head is the habitual object of exceptional pity. And why should I expect the truth from a go-between? Answer me, you rogue! What salamander has scorched your eyebrows?[13] What god do you dedicate your hair-crop to? Speak up, drug-fiend!'

108   I was numb with horror at the thought of punishment, and too confused to say anything when the case was so convincing. We were hideous. With shaven heads, and eyebrows as bald as our scalps, there was nothing to say and nothing to do. But when a damp sponge was wiped over my tear-stained face, when the ink dissolved all over my features and naturally enough blurred every line into a sooty cloud, his anger then doubled into fury.

Eumolpus protested that he would not see anyone sully freeborn men against all law and equity, and he rebutted the angry sailors' threats not only with words but with his fists. Our champion had his man at his side, and one or two passengers so sickly that they served as moral support rather than force in aid. And I was not asking for mercy myself; I waved my fists in Tryphaena's face, and declared in a clear, high voice that I would resort to physical violence unless she stopped ill-treating Giton, as she had a criminal mentality and was the only one of the whole shipload who deserved a thrashing. My boldness excited Lichas to wrath; he was furious that I should drop my own case and advocate somebody else's. Tryphaena flared up in equal rage at my abuse, and divided the entire ship into factions. On

one side, Eumolpus' man armed himself with a razor and handed us
out the rest of the blades, on the other Tryphaena's slaves put up
their bare fists, and even her maids roused the battlefield with cries.
The pilot was the only man left at his post, and he swore he would
abandon the helm if the madness provoked by the whim of a set of
outcasts did not end. The struggle raged on nevertheless; they
fought for revenge while we fought for our lives.

There were many casualties on both sides, but none fatal. Even
more combatants, bloody and wounded, retired just as if it were a
real pitched battle. And yet the fury on either side did not abate.
Then Giton valiantly turned his ugly razor on himself and threatened to lop off the part that had caused all our troubles. Tryphaena
staved off this monstrous deed by openly manifesting her pardon. I
myself had put my cut-throat to my neck several times, with no
more intention of suicide than Giton had of carrying out his threat.
And he played his tragedy all the more boldly knowing he wielded
the famous razor which he had already held to his throat.

The fight seemed to be taking an unusual turn, and the two sides
stood ready, when with some difficulty the pilot argued
Tryphaena into effecting a truce, like a real military envoy. After
an exchange of promises in traditional style, she took an olive-
branch from the ship's figurehead and held it out, and then braved
us by coming up to say:

> What fury turns peace into war? What crime is on our hands?
> In this ship no Trojan hero bears a prize beguiled from Atreus'
> son, nor does a raging Medea[14] fight with her brother's kin, but
> it is love despised that gives you strength. Ah! Is death to be
> courted at sea by drawn weapons? Who has not enough with
> his own single death?
>
>> Do not surpass the ocean, do not heap
>> Fresh floods of gore upon its savage deep.

The woman delivered this in a loud, emotional voice. The 109
fighting came to a momentary standstill, we suspended hostilities
and resumed our peaceable occupations. Our captain Eumolpus,
seizing on this sympathetic lull, first reproached Lichas vehemently
and then drew up and signed a treaty on these lines: 'You,
Tryphaena, by honour and by conscience bound, promise to
overlook all injuries done to you by Giton, and anything that took

place before this day shall not be held against him, nor shall he be
punished for it, nor shall it be pursued in any manner; and you shall
demand nothing of the boy contrary to his proper will and consent,
neither embrace, nor kiss, nor intimate sexual relations, under pain
and penalty of one hundred pieces cash down for each infringe-
ment. Furthermore, Lichas, by honour and by conscience bound,
you promise not to pursue Encolpius with insulting words or
offensive looks, and not to enquire where he sleeps by night, in
default whereof two hundred pieces cash down shall be paid for
each offence.'

A treaty was concluded on these terms, and we laid down our
arms. It was agreed we should bury the past with embraces all round,
in case any anger still lurked in our hearts even after the oath. Our
hatred collapsed amid general bonhomie, and a feast that had been
brought for the fight welded us in high good spirits. The whole ship
resounded with song, and as an unexpected calm had interrupted
our progress, we had one man who tried to harpoon the leaping fish,
and another who hauled in his wriggling prey with alluring hooks.
Even the sea-birds had come to perch on our yard-arms, and a clever
fowler reached them with a rod woven of reeds. They stuck to these
limed twigs and were delivered into our hands. Their down flut-
tered off and was caught by the breeze, and their feathers were
whirled over the surface of the sea by the insubstantial foam.

Lichas had already started being friendly with me again, and
already Tryphaena was blessing Giton by sprinkling the dregs of
her drink on him, when Eumolpus, the worse for wine, tried to
aim a few squibs at us bald and branded ones. His congealed wit
exhausted, he went back to his own poetry and began reciting this
Elegy on Hair:

> Our hair, sole crown of beauty, had to drop,
> Dim winter usurped the springtime crop;
> Our temples mourn their ravished shades,
> Smooth sunburnt brows laugh on lost blades.
> O perfidy! O gods! Your foremost gift,
> Pride of young days, is the first you lift.
>
> Wretch! Your hair shone more beautiful and bright
> Than Phoebus by day, and Phoebe by night!
> Now more polished than bronze, or the puffball

That rises after garden rainfall,
You shun and dread the girls who deride.
Death comes, believe me, in his long stride;
You ought to know your head
Already is part dead.

I think he wanted to go on and excel himself in silliness, but 110
Tryphaena's maid took Giton on the lower deck and dressed him up
in one of madame's wigs. Not only that, but she took some
eyebrows out of a box, and by shrewdly adjusting them on the lines
left by his sacrifice, she completely restored his beauty. Tryphaena
recognised the true Giton, and was moved to tears. Then she kissed
the boy with all her heart for the first time. Although I was glad to
see him returned to his former loveliness, I kept my own face out of
sight as much as I could, for I felt myself marked by a special
deformity, since even Lichas would not condescend to speak to me.
But the same maid rescued me from my dejection; she took me on
one side and fitted me with a head of hair as elegant as Giton's. More
so – my face shone to advantage, for my curly wig was golden.

*   *   *

Then Eumolpus, our standby in trouble and the author of our
present peace, started a series of taunts at the fickleness of women,
in case our high spirits flagged for want of a tale; how easily they
fell head over heels in love, how soon they forgot their own sons,
and how no woman was so modest that a strange new passion
could not turn her head to sheer folly. Without going back to
classical tragedies or to names notorious through the ages, he was
prepared to tell us, if we wanted to hear it, a story that took place
within living memory. So all eyes and ears were fixed on him, and
he began like this.

'There was a married woman of Ephesus[15] so famous for her 111
virtue that women came even from neighbouring lands to stare at
her. Now when her husband died, she was not content with the
ordinary custom of following the cortège with her hair down, or of
beating her breast in front of the assembled mourners. No, she
followed the dead man right to his last home, and when he had
been placed in a sepulchre like a Greek, began a watch on his body,
and wept over it by night and by day. Neither her parents nor her

relations could divert her from her fixed purpose or from tempting death by starvation. Finally, even the officials were rebuffed and went away.

'She was now passing her fifth day without food, lamented by all as a woman of unprecedented character. A devoted maid sat beside the sick woman and mingled sympathetic tears, renewing the lamp in the tomb every time it failed. The whole city talked of this and nothing else, and high and low alike agreed that here was love and virtue in one true and shining example.

'About this time the governor of the province ordered some thieves to be crucified next to the very tomb in which the woman mourned her loss. The night after, the soldier guarding the crosses against anyone who might tear down a body and bury it, noticed a bright light among the tombs, and heard sighs of mourning. Common human weakness made him long to know who it was and what was going on. So he went down to the sepulchre. He saw a woman of great beauty, and at first he was rooted in confusion, struck as if by some wonder or apparition from the underworld. When he saw the corpse stretched out, when he considered her tears and her face lacerated by her nails, he realised, as indeed was true, that the woman's grief for her lost man was unbearable.

'He fetched his supper into the tomb, and urged the mourner not to pursue her useless sorrow, nor to break her heart in unavailing anguish. For all mankind there is the same fate, the same last home, he said, and added the rest of the commonplaces that serve to restore the distressed mind to health. She ignored his consoling remarks, and beat and tore more violently at her breast, pulled out her hair and laid it on the body. The soldier did not retreat. By like encouragement, he tried to give the poor woman food, until the maid, undoubtedly seduced by the aroma of wine, gave in first and stretched out a hand to his courteous invitation.

'Refreshed by food and drink, she then assailed her stubborn mistress. "And what good would it do you," she said, "if you starved to death? Or if you buried yourself alive? Or if you surrendered your soul to Fate still unconsigned and before its due time? Do you believe the ashes care for that, or the spirits of the dead and buried? Why don't you begin life again? Shake off this feminine frailty and enjoy the pleasures of life as long as you may. This very body lying here ought to remind you that you should live."

'No one turns a deaf ear when urged to eat or to live. The woman, parched by so many days of abstinence, allowed her obstinacy to be overcome. She ate with as hearty an appetite as her maid, who had yielded first. I needn't tell you what temptation 112 usually preys on a well-replenished being. By the same allurements he used to ensure her will to live, the soldier now brought about an attack on her modesty. The good woman saw him to be handsome and well-spoken. To procure her favour, the maid was quoting, "Will you fight against a love that pleases?"[16] Why should I keep you in suspense? She couldn't abstain even from that part of the body, and the triumphant soldier captured it too.

'So they lay down together, and not only on that night did they take their pleasure, but on the following and the third night. Of course, the doors of the tomb were fastened; whoever came up to it, stranger or not, would think that this most virtuous widow had breathed her last on the body of her man. Well, the soldier was overjoyed with the beauty of his mistress and with their secret. He bought all the good things his resources allowed, and carried them into the tomb after dark.

'Then the parents of one of the crucified men, noticing the watch had relaxed, took down their hanged body at night and administered the last rites. The soldier, outwitted while off duty, saw on the following day that one cross lacked a body. He was afraid of punishment and told his mistress what had happened. He said he wouldn't wait for a sentence at law, but would punish his negligence with his own sword. She could oblige him with a place of burial after he had perished, letting him share the fatal tomb with her husband.

'As kind as she was modest, the woman cried, "The gods forbid that I should witness at the same time the deaths of the two men dearest to me! I would rather see a dead man hung up than a live one struck down!"

After this declaration she ordered her husband to be raised out of the coffin and fixed to the vacant cross. The soldier put the ingenuity of this most sagacious of women into effect, and the next day people were staggered at the way a dead man returned to his cross.'

The sailors guffawed at this story. Tryphaena blushed to the ears 113 and nuzzled a loving face in Giton's neck. But no laugh came from Lichas. He shook his head angrily and said, 'If the governor had been just, he would have replaced the husband's body in the tomb, and crucified the woman.'

No doubt his mind went back to Hedyle and how his ship was ransacked on her pleasure-cruise.[17] But the articles of the treaty did not permit him to rake up the past, and the gaiety that filled our hearts crowded out all resentment. By now Giton had Tryphaena on his lap, and now she covered his breast with kisses, now she adjusted her curls on his denuded head. I was in a fret, I was impatient with the new treaty, I could take no food or drink; I could only glower at the pair of them with wild, sidelong looks. Every kiss wounded me, every trick the depraved woman could invent. And still I did not know whether I was more angry with the boy for taking my mistress from me, or my mistress for corrupting my boy. Both things were most objectionable to my sight, and sadder far than my former captivity. What was more, Tryphaena no longer spoke to me as an intimate, as the lover she had been so pleased to have, and Giton did not think it worth his while to drink my health as usual, or, the very least he could do, admit me to the general conversation. I think he was afraid of opening a newly-healed scar just as they were patching up their friendship. Tears of misery welled from my heart, a sigh overwhelmed a groan that almost snatched my soul away . . .

*　　*　　*

He tried to cut in[18] and share our pleasures, not as a high and mighty master, but pestering for the favours of a friend.

*　　*　　*

'If you had a drop of good blood in you,[19] you would think no more of her than of an old bag. If you were a man you would lay off this whore.'

*　　*　　*

Nothing made me feel more ashamed than that Eumolpus might hit upon the whole situation, and that he would avenge himself in verse with a sharp-edged wit.

*　　*　　*

Eumolpus swore an oath in the most formal terms.

*　　*　　*

While we were discussing all these things, the sea heaved, and 114
clouds gathered from every point to throw a dark pall upon the
day. Sailors ran feverishly to their posts and took in the sails before
the storm. But the wind veered constantly, and the pilot had no
idea which course to hold. Sometimes the wind set for Sicily; far
more often the north wind that prevails along the Italian coasts
sheered the vessel round this way and that at its whim and, more
dangerous than any tempest, a sudden, thick darkness shut out the
light, and the helmsman could not make out the prow. Then, if
you please, with the storm at its height, Lichas trembled and
stretched out his hands to entreat me: 'Encolpius, help us in our
distress. Give the ship back her sacred robe and rattle.[20] By all the
gods, have mercy on us, just as you always used to.'

But as he cried these words the wind canted him overboard. A
squall spun him round and round in a treacherous whirlpool that
sucked him under. Meanwhile, Tryphaena's devoted servants almost forced her into a boat with the better part of her baggage, and
saved her from certain death. I clung to Giton, I wept and cried, 'Is
this all we deserve from the gods, that they unite us in death alone?
But Fate cruelly refuses even that. Look, the waves are ready to
capsize the ship, and now the raging sea is about to tear two close-
locked lovers apart. So if your love for Encolpius was a true love, kiss
him while you can, and snatch a last joy from our coming doom.'

As I said this Giton undressed, and covering himself with my
shirt, raised his head to be kissed. He buckled his belt tightly round
our two bodies so that no envious wave should separate us as we
clung together, and said, 'If nothing else, at least we shall be united
for an infinity while the sea bears us off, and if she takes pity and
casts us up on the same shore, perhaps some passer-by in simple
humanity will cover us with a few stones, or perhaps in a crowning
labour that even the callous waves cannot forgo, they will bury us
beneath unconscious sands.'

I accepted his last bond, and like a man arrayed upon his
deathbed, I waited for an end that had now lost its sting.

In the meantime the storm went about the business of Fate and
battered off the remains of the ship. There was no mast, no rudder,
no rigging, no oars, but something like a crude and shapeless hulk
that drifted with the wave.

*   *   *

Fishermen put out to sea in light craft to plunder the wreck, but when they saw men aboard ready to defend their belongings, their barbarous scheme switched to an offer of help.

*   *   *

115 We heard a strange mutter below the master's cabin and a moaning as of a wild beast that wanted to break loose. We followed the noise and found Eumolpus seated there scrawling verses over a huge piece of parchment. We could scarcely believe he had time to compose poetry when death was lurking, so we hauled him out, not without protest, and insisted on his being reasonable. He was furious at this interruption, and said, 'Let me finish my phrase, the poem has a lame ending.'

I laid hands on the idiot, and had Giton help me drag the bellowing poet ashore.

*   *   *

When this rather difficult operation was over, we retired to a fisherman's hut. Our hearts were heavy. We refreshed ourselves indifferently with some food spoilt by sea-water, and passed a night of utter misery. In the morning, as we were deciding which way we might venture, I suddenly caught sight of a human body rolling in a slight undertow that carried it to the shore. The sight held me; I saddened, and turned moist eyes to the treacherous sea.

'Perhaps,' I cried, 'a wife in some distant land waits cheerfully for this man, perhaps a son ignorant of the storm, or a father, or someone at least to whom he gave his farewell kiss. So much for scheming mortals! So much for the cravings of vast ambition! So this is how man keeps his head above water!'

Up to now I had been lamenting a stranger, and then a wave turned shoreward a face that was as yet unravaged.

I saw it was Lichas, terrible and unrelenting but a short while ago, and now virtually cast at my feet. Then I could restrain my tears no longer, and I struck my breast again and again.

'Oh, where is your anger now?' I cried. 'Your tyranny, where is it? Here, here you are, a prey to fish and monsters of the deep. Not long ago you boasted of the power at your command, and yet of all your great ship you have not even the shipwrecked man's one plank. Go now, mortal men, swell your hearts with ambitious

plans! Go, misers, invest for a thousand years the riches won by
fraud! This man here looked into the accounts of his estate
yesterday, and even settled on what day he would return home. O
gods, gods, see how far he lies from his own true end! But it is not
only the high seas that offer man treachery. The warrior is betrayed
by his weapons; this man, as he makes offerings to the gods, is
buried when his house collapses on him; that man is thrown from
his carriage and has his brains dashed out for his haste. A glutton
chokes at table, a cheese-paring man dies in a fast. When you
consider it all, shipwreck is everywhere. You say a man lost at sea
has no burial. But what does it matter to fleshly remains how they
are consumed, whether by fire, water, or the decay of time? Do
what you will, the end is always the same. But, you protest, wild
beasts will tear his flesh to pieces! As though fire gave some kindlier
welcome! When we are angry with our slaves, do we not think fire
the cruellest punishment? Then what folly it is to spare no pains in
having every scrap of us buried!'

*   *   *

And so Lichas was burned on the funeral pyre raised by his
enemies' hands. Eumolpus composed an epitaph for the dead man,
casting his eyes high and wide for inspiration.

*   *   *

We willingly performed this last office, and then followed the route   116
we had chosen. In a short while we had sweated our way to the top
of a mountain, and from here we caught sight of a town, set on a
height, and at no great distance. We had strayed too far to know the
name, but a countryman gave us to understand it was Croton, a
town of high antiquity,[21] and once the first in all Italy. When we
questioned him with some curiosity as to what men lived on this
distinguished soil, and what kind of business particularly flourished
now that a succession of wars had drained their wealth, he said, 'My
friends, if you are businessmen, change your plans, and look for
some other means of support. But if you can keep up appearances as
men of breeding and out-and-out liars, you will be running head
first into money. For in this town they have no respect for learning,
fine speaking has no place here, temperance and the good life do
not come in for the honour that is their due; in fact you should

know that the whole male population of the town is divided into two classes: they are either legacy-makers or legacy-hunters. Nobody raises a family here, for anybody with heirs of his own breeding is debarred from public amusements and dinner-parties, is deprived of all privileges and must languish among the outcasts. On the other hand, the man who has never taken a wife and has no close relatives may reach the peak of social honours; only such men are military geniuses, and they alone lead courageous and blameless lives. You are entering a town,' he went on, 'that can be likened to a plague-stricken plain, where nothing can be found but half-eaten bodies, and the vultures that feed on them.'

*   *   *

117 Eumolpus applied his cautious mind to the new situation, and confessed that this kind of moneymaking did not displease him. I thought our ancient was joking, some poetic banter, but then he added, 'I wish I had a more ample setting, I mean some clothes of better cut, to lend my make-believe an air of veracity. No, I swear I won't put it off until tomorrow; I'll lead you right away to the fortune of your lives.'

Anyhow, I promised to do whatever he demanded, provided he was satisfied with the clothes that had been with us in our foraging, and with whatever we found in Lycurgus' villa when we broke in.[22]

'And as for ready money for present needs, the mother of the gods[23] will pay up most loyally.'

'Well then,' said Eumolpus, 'why delay rehearsing our act? Appoint me master if it suits you.'

There was nothing to lose, and no one dared criticise the plot. To safeguard the imposture among ourselves, we took an oath of obedience to Eumolpus; to suffer burning, imprisonment, flogging, death by the sword, and anything else he ordered. Like thoroughgoing gladiators, we dedicated our bodies and souls in all solemnity to our new master. When the oath was made, we put on our slave's clothing and hailed him. Then we learnt from Eumolpus that he had just lost a son, a young man of unusual eloquence and with a great future, which was why the broken-hearted old man had left his own country, not to have his son's dependants and friends in sight, not, above all, the tomb that caused his tears day after day. His recent shipwreck only added to this misery, and he had lost more than two million in it; not that it was so much the loss that hurt him, but that no one would recognise his true rank without his servants. Over and above this, he had thirty million tied up in African properties and investments; and as for slaves, he had such hordes scattered through the fields of Numidia he could have taken Carthage if he had wanted to. To adumbrate this skeleton plan we recommended Eumolpus to cough excessively, or at least to have stomach ulcers and condemn every variety of food in front of everybody. All his talk must be gold and silver, estates run at a loss, and the never-ending barrenness of the soil. Further, he was to sit over his accounts day in and day out, and revise the clauses of his will every month. And to complete the tableau, every time he wanted to call one of us, he was to confuse our names, and so let it be clearly seen that the master had more of us in mind than were on the spot.

We ordered these matters, offered a prayer to the gods for success and happiness, and struck out on our way. But Giton could not bear his burden, being unused to it, and Corax the manservant, a real dodger of work, put his bundle down as often as possible, damned our speed, and swore he would either throw away our packs or make off with his own load.

'Eh, d'you take me for a pack-mule,' he complained, 'or a stone-barge? I was hired as a man, not a horse. I'm just as much a freeman as any of you, even if my father did leave me poor.'

Cavilling was not enough for him, and he would keep lifting his leg to fill the road with an objectionable noise and smell. His insolence made Giton laugh and mimic by mouth each breaking of wind.

* * *

'How many of our young men,' argued Eumolpus, 'have been inveigled by poetry. No sooner has one of them marshalled a verse into feet and has complicated a sentimental thought with a circumlocution than, why, he thinks he has scaled Helicon[24] in one move. So many who are tired out with the grind of the law courts take refuge in the calm of poetry as if it were some kindlier harbour, supposing it easier to compose an epic than a declamation studded with glittering maxims. But men of quality do not love such idle

118

vanities, and the mind cannot conceive and bear forth unless
flooded from the vast reservoir of literature. A man must avoid all,
so to speak, cut-price diction, and choose his words from outside
colloquial use; his motto is, "I hate the common mob, and hold
it off."[25]

'Besides, he must take care that his epigrams do not stand out
from the body of the work; they must be woven into the material
and shine with like colours. Witness Homer and the lyricists,
Roman Virgil, and Horace with his studied felicity. The others
have either not seen the road that leads to poetry, or have done so
and were afraid to tread it. We have the tremendous subject of the
Civil War; whoever attempts it and is not thoroughly well-read
will give way under the weight. For it is not a matter of wrapping
up current events in verses, a thing the historians could do far
better, but the imagination should so soar through symbolism,
divine intervention, and an agony of mythological terms, that the
result must seem more like the prophetic frenzy of a mind inspired
than a scrupulous account attested on oath. If you would like to
hear it, the following improvisation is an example, although it has
not had the final touches:

119   'Now the whole world was the Roman conqueror's.[26] He held
        the sea, the land, and the coursing firmament, but this was not
        enough. His laden ships disturbed the foaming waters, and if
        there remained beyond some undiscovered bay, a country rich
        in yellow gold, here was an enemy, here destiny hatched the
        disasters of war as they searched for their wealth. Familiar joys
        grew stale, and common pleasures dull. The seaborne soldier
        praised Corinthian bronze, and purple itself dimmed before
        lustres worked from underground; Africans cursed Rome, the
        Chinese brought new silks, and all Arabia ransacked its
        countryside.

        Then new diseases fall to wound a stricken peace. They hunt
        the woodland beast for gold, and penetrate as far as Hammon's
        lands in Africa to win the monster whose murderous teeth are
        so precious. Strange, ravenous creatures are freighted in their
        vessels; a pacing tiger rides in a gilded cage, and laps to please
        the roaring crowd.

        Alas, I am ashamed to speak and reveal the fate that falls upon

them. It is a Persian custom; they abduct young boys, scarcely
of years; the mutilating steel condemns them all to lust, and in
this bid to stay the hurrying years and delay swift-changing age,
Nature seeks her natural way and cannot find it. So for pleasure
every man has a minion, with effeminate body and mincing
gait, with flowing hair and heaps of novel-sounding clothes,
the very things to entice a man.

And now they root from African soil tables of citrus-wood,
patterned like vulgar gold, with a polish reflecting hosts of
slaves and purple. It makes the senses whirl. About this sterile
wood, ignobly rare, a pressing crowd is swamped with wine. A
mercenary soldier eats the whole world's produce; his arms are
rust. The belly is a subtle force; the parrot-fish, plunged in
Sicilian brine, is brought to the table alive; oysters come
ravished from the banks of Lucrine Lake, at a price, and whet
the appetite while they drain the purse. Now the birds are all
gone from the waters of Phasis, the shore is dumb, and the
hollow winds whisper in the empty boughs.

Public madness is the same. The citizen is bought, he votes
for plunder, for whoever rattles gold. They are corrupt, the
senate is corrupt, their favour has a price. Even old men decay
in liberty and virtue; power shifts ground as money passes, and
their gold-tainted grandeur lies rotten in the dust.

Cato is struck and spurned; his victor, more wretched than
he, can only blush to seize the rods of office from Cato's hands.
For the people's shame and ruined character lay not so much in
the defeat of one man, but that in that man fell the might and
glory of Rome; then was Rome a ruined city, at once the price
and the unredeemable goods.

Moreover, the people sank in a twin slough of horrid usury
and all-devouring debts. No home is safe, not a soul but is
mortgaged; the soft decay is born in the silent marrow and
spreads raging through the limbs in full cry. They take to their
weapons like desperate men, and the goods they squandered in
luxury, they now seek in bloody wounds. Deep in this filth, far
gone in this slumber, what remedy could wake a Rome but
terror, war, and lusting steel?

Now Fortune reared three leaders, and the Goddess of War 120
buried them each apart under a trophy of arms. The Parthians

keep Crassus, Pompey lies by Libya's sea, Caesar shed his blood
in ungrateful Rome. Their ashes lie wide, as if the earth itself
could scarcely hold so many graves; such are the honours
conferred by fame.

There is a place plunged deep in a gaping cleft between
Parthenope and great Dicarchis' fields, flooded by the water of
Cocytus. The wild fumes that rush from it spread seething
mortality. Here the country knows no autumn green, the field
is never rich with turf or herb, never the thickets hum with
springtime song in gentle discrepancy, but chaos and parched
black pumice-rocks rejoice only in the funereal cypress that
mounts above. In this place the father of Dis raised his hand,
burning with funeral fires and white with scattered ashes, and
challenged winged Fortune with these words: "O Chance, you
in whose power all human things and divine are, ill-pleased
with might that stays too long secure, ever loving the new, ever
quick to dispose of a gain, do you not feel crushed beneath the
weight of Rome, can you not heave the mass that should perish?
The youth of Rome despise their own strength, and cannot
bear their fabric of wealth. See, on all sides the glut of spoils is
lavished, and giddy fortunes bring them doom. They build in
gold and make their mansions touch the stars, they dash back
the waters with piers and flood the fields, and flout the elements
to reverse the order of things. They hammer at my kingdom
too. The earth is yawning with insane excavations, and mountains are levelled until the very caves groan. And as they quarry
stones, devoid of purpose, the very ghosts of hell proclaim their
hopes of reaching heaven. Then, Chance, do this: change a
peaceful to a warlike face, stir the Romans to enrich my realm
with their dead. Too long it is since my mouth dripped with
human blood, and long since my Tisiphone bathed her thirsty
limbs in it; not since Sulla's sword drank deep and the whole
earth bristled with blood-fattened crops in the sun."

121   He spoke, and tried to grasp her right hand in his, and so rent
the earth in two. Then Fortune answered lightly: "O Father,
whom the furthest reaches of Cocytus obey, your wishes shall
come true, if I may safely reveal the future. For a wrath like
yours seethes in my heart, and as fierce a flame eats to my core;
my gifts anger me, I hate all I gave Rome and her citadels. The

god who piled these heights shall bring them low; my heart
yearns to have men burned and gorge their blood. Already I see
the plain of Philippi littered with the dead of two battles, I see
pyres ablaze in Thessaly, and the funeral rites of the Spanish
race. Already the clash of arms resounds in my anxious ears. I
see your barriers, O Nile, groan in Libya, I see the horror of the
gulf of Actium, and Apollo's army. Come, open your thirsty
lands, and welcome fresh souls! Charon can scarcely ferry the
warrior-ghosts; it is work for a fleet! And you, pale Tisiphone,
glut yourself on measureless ruin, suck the wounds you hacked
wide open. All the world is rags, and hurries down to the
Stygian shades."

She was no sooner finished than the cloud shook, and rent   122
with flashing lightning, shot out its flame. The Father of
Darkness recoiled, and at his brother's thunderbolt he closed
the lap of the earth in panic. At once the gods made plain by
signs disasters and destructions to come: Titan, misshapen,
bloody-faced, withdrew to darkness, as though already he
sensed the civil strife. Elsewhere Cynthia quenched her full
orb, and would not light the crime. Mountain peaks cracked
and their slopes thundered, and waters strayed from familiar
banks to expire. The clash of arms raged to the sky, a trumpet
shivered the constellations and woke up Mars. Soon Etna is
devoured with unusual fires, and jets her meteors high. Among
the tombs, among the bones that cried for burial, the faces of
the dead menace with horrid shrieks. A comet with a company
of unknown stars spreads fire, and Jupiter comes down in a
shower of blood. The god soon makes these portents plain. For
Caesar shakes off all delay, and moved by love of vengeance,
throws down his arms in Gaul to take up civil war.

High in the sky-touched Alps, where the Greek god trod the
rocks that now slope down to let men come and go, there is a
place sacred to the altars of Hercules; winter locks it with rigid
snow, and raises its hoar-white head to the stars. It is as if the sky
recoils; it never softens under mellow sunshine or the breath of
vernal winds, but stiffens with thick ice and winter frost,
louring shoulders that might bear the whole world. When
Caesar marched to these mountains with his triumphant army
and chose his camp, he looked across the Italian plains from the

height of a peak, and with a high voice, with both hands raised
to the stars, he said: "Almighty Jupiter, and you, land of Saturn,
once heartened by my victories and laden with my triumphs,
bear witness that reluctantly I beckon Mars to battle that my
hands unwillingly engage. But my wounds compel me, my
banishment from that City, even while I stain the Rhine with
blood, and turn back the Gauls as they march a second time on
Rome, for victory only made my exile more sure. It was
German blood and my sixty victories that made me an offender.
Yet who fears my renown, who are they who watch me fight?
Low hirelings with their price, to whom my Rome is step-
mother. But not, I think, with impunity, for no cowards shall
bind my arm without my due revenge. Then forward, my men,
forward in victory and fury, and plead my cause with steel! One
charge is cried against us all, and for all one disaster is ready. My
gratitude is due to you, I did not conquer alone! And since
punishment threatens our trophies, and our victory deserves
humiliation, cast the die and let Fortune decide. Engage the
war, and test your strength! My plea has been heard; armed
with such might I cannot know defeat."

He cried the words aloud, and from the sky the Delphic
raven gave a glad omen, and beat the air in flight. And from the
left of a forbidding wood came strange words, and after them
flames. Phoebus in his orb glowed larger and brighter, and
wreathed his face with a golden halo.

123   Caesar took heart from all these omens. He advanced the
standards of Mars, and displayed his daring by an unsurpassed
march. The ice and hoar-white frost that bound the earth
were no foes at first, but lay quiet in their cold, yet when the
troops broke through the close-knit clouds, the shying horse
cracked the fettered waters, and the snow melted. Soon
newborn rivers rolled from the mountain-tops, but even
stayed their course as by command; the waves froze as they
fell, and that thaw turned hard enough to hack. Uncertain
before, the ice now baffled their steps and tricked their feet;
regiments, men and arms lay heaped in wretched confusion.
The clouds then, buffeted by freezing gales, discharged their
waters, whirlwinds were unleashed, and the sky broke into
prodigious hail. The very clouds fell piecemeal on the army,

a solid ice flattened on them like a breaker from the sea. The
earth was vanquished by immeasurable snows; vanquished the
stars in the sky; vanquished the rivers motionless by their
banks. But Caesar was not conquered, and, leaning on his tall
spear, he crossed these dreadful regions with unwavering step,
even as the son of Amphitryon came down from the steep
Caucasian citadel, or as Jupiter with his fierce eyes when he
descended from the heights of Olympus to scatter the weapons
of the ill-fated Giants.

While Caesar in anger trod down these insolent heights,
terror-stricken Rumour beat her wings and flew to find proud
Palatine hill; she struck the images of all the gods with this
Roman thunderbolt: "Now the fleet scours the sea, and the
Alps seethe with legions bathed in German blood."

Arms, blood, slaughter, fire, the whole of war surged before
their eyes. Their hearts beat fearfully, and terror divides them
between two courses; this man would prefer retreat by land, the
other, flight by sea, the open sea now safer than his country.
Another would fight and submit to Fate's decrees. Fear sends
each flying so far as her grip ensures. In this flux even the people
hastily abandon the city and go where panic leads them, a
miserable sight. Rome is pleased to desert, and abashed citizens
quit sorrowful homes at the mere breath of rumour. One
clutches children with a trembling hand, another conceals
household gods next to his heart, leaves his door in tears, and in
his prayers wills death to the distant enemy. There are those
who crush wives to their mourning hearts, and youths who
bear the strange burden of their aged sires. Each drags away
what he most fears to lose. One thoughtlessly takes all his goods
with him bringing booty direct to the battle. So it is when the
great south wind blows up from the high seas and whips the
waters, and neither rigging nor the helm avail the crew; one
lashes stout planks of pine, another has hopes of a sheltered bay
and a tranquil shore, a third puts on all sail to fly and trusts in
chance. But why lament these lesser griefs? With the other
consul, Pompey the Great, the terror of Pontus, explorer of the
wild Hydaspes, scourge of pirates, whose triple acclamation
made Jupiter tremble, he who was revered when he broke the
raging swirl of the Euxine Sea and subdued the waters of the

Bosphorus, he, Pompey, in all his shame, fled the very name of power, that indifferent Fortune might see the back of Pompey the Great.

124   The vast contagion spread to the gods; panic in heaven answered the mortal rout. See, throughout the world mild deities forsake the brawling earth and detest it, and turn their faces from the van of doomed humanity. First among all others, Peace stirred her snow-white limbs and hid a vanquished head beneath her helmet, leaving the world in flight for iron Pluto's realm. With her went Faith, dejected, wild-haired Justice, and weeping Concord, her dress rent to pieces. But the wide-gaping earth revealed where Erebus dwelled, and here by contrast rose from far Pluto's ministers, a dreadful Fury, aggressive Bellona, Megaera armed with firebrands, Destruction, the Ambuscades, and the livid form of Death. Among them Fury, unleashed and uncontrolled, raised high her bloody head, and covered her face, pitted by a thousand wounds, with a gory helmet. The battered shield of Mars hung on her left arm, bristling, heavily stuck with numberless spearheads, and her right hand shook a flaming brand that threatened fire throughout the world.

The earth felt the weight of the gods. The constellations drooped and vainly sought their gravities: the whole court of heaven fell into two camps. First Venus championed Caesar's cause, then Pallas is at her side, then Romulus, wielding a mighty spear. Great Pompey has Diana and Mercury, and Hercules of Tiryns, so like him in his deeds.

The trumpets quivered, and wild-haired Discord lifted her Stygian head to the gods above. Her face was clotted with blood, her swollen eyes ran with tears, her brazen teeth were scurfed with rust, her slavering tongue dripped, her features were choked with snakes, her twisted breasts hid in a tattered dress, her shaking right hand waved a blood-red torch. She left the shadows of Cocytus and Tartarus and made for high on the proud Appennines, here to survey every land and shore, and armies pouring through the world. This cry broke from her savage breast: "People, take arms while your hearts are wrathful, to arms! Set your torches to the cities' midst! The coward shall perish; let none waver, women or children, or the old who are desolate with age. Let the earth tremble, your shattered roof-tops rebel! You, Marcellus, keep law and order. Curio, encourage the people. You, Lentulus, forward the hardy deeds of Mars. Why do you hesitate to do battle, Caesar? Why no breaking of doors, no destruction of city walls, why are you not looting treasures? And does not Pompey know how to defend the ramparts of Rome? Let him try for the walls of Dyrrachium, and stain the bays of Thessaly with human blood."

And it was on earth as Discord commanded.'

6

Encolpius' amorous adventures at Croton

Eumolpus poured out his words with breathtaking fluency, and at last we entered Croton. We refreshed ourselves at an unpretentious inn, and the next day, looking for a house that was better appointed, we fell in with a group of legacy-hunters who were curious to know what sort of men we were and where we came from. We acted, as we had all agreed, on a preconcerted plan, and answered these questions with such an overwhelming gush of words that they readily believed us. Without further ado they were fiercely contesting as to who should shower his personal wealth on Eumolpus.

*   *   *

All the legacy-hunters solicited Eumolpus' favour with presents.

*   *   *

This went on in Croton for a long time . . . and Eumolpus, bloated with success, so far forgot his old life as to boast that there was no one on whom his benign influence did not fall, and if they committed any crime in that town, they would go free by the good offices of his friends. But though day after day I stuffed myself to plumpness on a mass of good things, ever and ever bigger, and had a notion that malignant Fate had turned her face away from me, yet I often gave as much thought to my past state as to my present well-being. I would say to myself, 'What if some cunning legacy-hunter sent a spy to Africa and found out our lie? What if Eumolpus' man[1] got tired of his current good luck, dropped a hint to his friends, and laid bare the whole imposture out of spiteful treachery? Only this: it would mean another running away, we would be beggars again, and would embrace a poverty we had finally overcome. Gods and

goddesses, what an ill-favoured thing it is to live without the law!
Always expecting just what you deserve!'

                          *   *   *

126 'Because you know your own sexual power, you are haughty, and
sell your caress instead of giving it. What point is there in your
combed and curly hair, your face caked with make-up, and those
melting, provoking eyes, that nicely-balanced walk which never
puts a foot wrong? Simply that you are advertising your beauty for
sale. Look at me – I know nothing of fortune-telling, I set no store
by the astrologer's chart, but I read characters in men's faces, and
when I see a man walk I know what is in his mind. Well, if you will
sell us what I want, you have a ready buyer. Or if you will be so
good as to present us with it, I shall be greatly obliged. When you
say you are a low slave[2] it only fans a smouldering desire. For there
are some women who are inflamed by the dregs, whose lust is only
roused by the sight of a slave or an attendant with his dress up.
Some are hot for gladiators, some for a dust-covered mule-driver,
or for an actor who exhibits himself on the stage. My mistress is
one of this type; she skips the fourteen rows from the orchestra[3]
and picks up a lover in the rabble at the back.'

I brimmed with joy at her seductive words and said, 'Please, the
person who loves me, could it be you?'

The maid laughed long and loud at this gauche approach, and then
said, 'Don't flatter yourself. No slave has ever gone to bed with me,
and if the gods are good I shall never put my arms round a gallows-
bird. Let the married ones who kiss the weals after a flogging do that.
Even if I am a maid, I only rub shoulders with knights.'

I gasped at such ill-assorted passions, and reckoned it a freak that
the maid should have the pride of a matron and the woman the low
tastes of a maid. Our pleasantries went on, and I asked the maid to
bring her mistress to the grove of plane trees. The girl agreed.
Picking up her skirt, she turned off into the clump of laurels that
grew close to our pathway. A minute later she produced the lady
from this hiding-place, and set beside me a creature more perfect
than any masterpiece. No words might comprehend her beauty,
and anything I say must of necessity fall short. Her hair curled
naturally and spread profusely on her shoulders; it swept back from
the roots, and her forehead was narrow. Her eyebrows curved to

the edge of her cheekbones, even so almost meeting between her eyes, and these flashed more brightly than stars remote from the orb of the moon. She had nostrils slightly flaring, and the mouth Praxiteles conceived for Diana.[4] And her chin, the nape of her neck, her hands, her glistening foot caught in a slender gold band! It outshone the marble of Paros.*[5] So I set aside my ancient love for Doris[6] for the first time.

* * *

> What can have happened, Jupiter?
> You throw down your arms;
> Silent among the heavenly host,
> You are an unspoken myth.
> Now is the time to sprout horns
> On your grim brow, now the time
> To hide grey hairs in swansdown.
> Here is the true Danaë.[7] Do but desire
> To touch her body, all your limbs
> Shall melt in liquid fire.

* * *

She was delighted, and smiled such a fetching smile that I thought I saw her face as the full moon breaking out of a cloud. She spoke, and the motion of her fingers led her voice eloquently along: 'If you do not despise a woman of quality who has experienced the opposite sex for the first time this year, then, young man, I bring you a sister.[8] You have, I know, a brother as well, for I did not hesitate to enquire, but why should you not gain a sister too? I come in the same capacity. Deign to know my kiss, that alone, and only at your pleasure.'

'Rather it is I who should ask you,' I replied, 'in the name of your beauty, not to scorn admitting a stranger among your devoted friends. You will find him a true believer if you permit him to worship you. And do not think I enter the Temple of Love empty-handed; I give you my own brother.'

'What?' she said. 'Sacrifice to me the one you cannot live without? On whose lips you hang, and whom you love as much as I want you to love me?'

While she spoke, her voice took on such a winning grace, so

gentle a sound caressed the swooning air, it seemed like the song of
the Sirens[9] borne harmoniously on the breeze. In my ecstasy the
whole light of the sky shone somehow more radiantly upon me,
and I asked to know the name of my goddess.

'So,' she said, 'my maid did not tell you that I am called Circe?
True, I am not the daughter of the Sun, nor did my mother delay
the course of the spinning world while she took her pleasure. But I
shall be indebted to the heavens if fate has brought us together. Yes,
I feel some kind of subtle, divine reasoning is at work. For Circe
loves Polyaenus with good reason;[10] a great flame is kindled whenever these two names meet. Take me in your arms if you want me.
Fear no spying eyes; your brother is far from this place.'

So spoke Circe, and putting two feather-soft arms around me, she
drew me down to the ground, carpeted with a thousand flowers.

> Such flowers our mother Earth did strew
> From Ida's peak, when joined in mutual love
> With Jupiter; his heart was utter fire.
> Glowing roses, violets, the modest galingale;
> The lily laughing white from the green meadow-grass.
> The yielding land invited Venus to its sward,
> The brighter day indulged their darker loves.

We were locked in one embrace on this bed of flowers, and
exchanged a thousand kisses, all with an eye to lusty pleasure.

*   *   *

128 'What is it?' she said.[11] 'Has my kiss put you off? Is my breath
offensive through fasting? Or is it some perspiration carelessly left
under my arms? If it is none of these things, is it, as I think, Giton
that you're afraid of?'

An obvious shame flushed my face red. If I had any hard
masculinity, I lost it now, and my whole body went limp.

'Oh please,' I cried, 'don't taunt me in my misery. I have been
drugged.'

*   *   *

'Tell me, Chrysis, tell me true. Am I ugly? Am I slovenly? Has
some natural defect blemished my beauty? Don't lie to your
mistress. I am to blame, but for what, I do not know.'

She snatched a mirror from her silent maid, and after trying all the smirks that usually occasion lovers' smiles she shook out her dress, crumpled by the ground, and sped to the temple of Venus. But I stood there like a man condemned, like someone who has seen a horrific sight, and I began to ask my conscience whether I had not been cheated of my true pleasure.

> When in the sleep-thick night so many dreams
> Mock our bewildered eyes, as when we dig
> The earth and light on gold, our wicked hands
> Caress the spoil, and snatch the treasure,
> Sweat soaks our face, and in our heart
> We fear someone will shake us knowingly,
> Our vest crammed full of secret gold. Soon
> The splendours vanish from our passive mind,
> Old, true shapes return, the heart is hot
> For what is gone, and runs sheerly through
> The brilliant shadows of remembered things.

*   *   *

'And so on this account I have to thank you for loving me with true Socratic detachment. Alcibiades in his master's bed[12] was never respected like this.'

*   *   *

'Believe me, brother, I do not realise I am a man, I don't feel it. The part of my body that made an Achilles of me[13] is dead and buried.'

*   *   *

The boy was afraid he would lay himself open to gossip if he were caught with me in private; he tore himself away, and fled to an inner room in the house.

*   *   *

But Chrysis came into my room and gave me a letter from her mistress. This is what she wrote: 'Circe to Polyaenus, greetings. If I were a sensual woman, I should complain that I had been deceived, but as it is I am grateful for your lethargy. I have idled

too long in the shadow of pleasure. But I would like to know how
you are, and whether you got home on your own two feet; the
doctors say men without sinews cannot walk. Let me tell you,
young man, beware of paralysis. I have never seen a sick man in
such great danger; upon my word, you are half dead already. If
this coldness gets to your knees and your hands, you may as well
send for the dead-march trumpeters. Well, what is to be done?
Even if I have been deeply insulted by you I cannot grudge a
remedy for so bad a case. If you want to get better, ask Giton. I say
you will recover your sinews if you sleep without your brother
for three nights. As for me, I am not afraid of finding someone
who likes me less. My mirror and my reputation do not lie. Keep
well, if you can.'

When Chrysis saw that I had read the whole complaint from end
to end she said, 'These things happen quite often, particularly in
this town, where there are witches who can bring down the moon
from the sky . . . and so this matter will be looked after too. Just
send a soothing reply to my mistress and restore her good spirits by
being frank and courteous. The truth is, since the time you insulted
her, she has not been quite herself.'

I cheerfully obeyed the girl, and wrote out this note on the
tablet: 'Polyaenus to Circe, greetings. I do admit, dear Madam, I
have often offended, for I am a man, and still a young one. And yet
until this day, I have never committed a deadly sin. You have a
culprit's confession; he deserves whatever punishment you order. I
have been a traitor, a homicide, I have committed sacrilege; insist
rightly on my punishment for these misdeeds. If you decide on my
death, I will come with my sword. If you are pleased to have me
flogged, I will run naked to my mistress. Remember only this: it
was not me, but my equipment that failed. The soldier was ready
for battle, and had no weapon. Who upset me I do not know.
Perhaps the spirit ran ahead of the lagging flesh, perhaps I aimed at
perfect satisfaction and wasted my passion by delay. What I did I
cannot tell. You advise me to look out for paralysis – as if there
could be something worse than the malady that deprived me of
possessing you! The sum total of my apology is this: I will do your
pleasure, if you let me mend my fault.'

*   *   *

Chrysis was sent off with these promises. I took great care of my importunate body, dispensed with the bath, and made do with a light rubbing-down. Then I fed on some rather strong food, onions, that is, and the heads of snails prepared without sauce, with a sparing draught of wine. I settled myself with a brief walk before bed and went to my room without Giton. I was so fastidious to please her that I dreaded the least touch of my brother.

The next day I got up as fresh in body as in mind, and went off 131 to the same grove of plane trees, although I was afraid of this unlucky spot, and began to wait under the trees for Chrysis to lead the way. After going round once or twice I sat down exactly where I was the day before, and then she appeared with a little old woman trailing behind.[14] She greeted me and said, 'So, squeamish one, can you stomach it now?'

The old woman drew a twist of different coloured threads from her dress and bound it round my neck. Then she mixed some dust with her spittle, put her middle finger in it, and made a mark in spite of my disgust . . .

When this was over she chanted an order: I was to spit three times and toss pebbles into my bosom three times, after she had cast a spell on them and wrapped them in purple. She brought her hands to bear on my member, and quicker than I can tell the sinew obeyed, and with a mighty leap filled the old woman's hands. Overcome with joy, she cried, 'You see, my dear Chrysis, what a hare I've started for the others?'

*   *   *

The lofty plane, the laurel bound with berries,
The quivering cypress spread a summer shade,
And the bare-trimmed pine-top shivered.
A foaming stream with idle water
Played among them, and jarred the pebbles
In chattering flow.
It was a place for love.
So proved the woodland nightingale,
So the swallow come from town,
As they skimmed the turf and violet soft
And shrined their hidden love in song.

*   *   *

Circe was resting, her marble neck pressed back on a gilded bed.
She fanned herself nonchalantly with a flowering spray of myrtle.
When she saw me she blushed a little, remembering yesterday's
insult, no doubt; then she sent everybody else away and had me sit
down beside her. She covered my eyes with the myrtle-spray and
grew bolder with this screen between us.

'Well, my paralytic,' she began, 'have you come here the complete man today?'

'Why ask me,' I answered, 'why not try?'

I threw myself utterly into her arms, and grew weary of her
abundant kisses, unfettered by any witchcraft.

*   *   *

132 The eloquent beauty of her body was an invitation to love itself.
Our lips bruised in a hundred fierce kisses, our clasped hands
devised all kinds of lovers' tricks, our bodies grew to a single
embrace that united our souls.

*   *   *

The lady was exasperated[15] by my flagrant insults. She turned to do
vengeance. She summoned her grooms and ordered me to be
flogged. And the woman was not satisfied with this gross outrage,
but called her seamstresses and the scum of the backstairs and had
them spit on me. I covered my eyes with my hands. I did not burst
out in any appeal, for I knew only too well what I deserved. Beaten
and bespattered, I was kicked out of doors. They threw out
Proselenus too, and thrashed Chrysis. Without exception, the
servants muttered moodily to themselves, asking what it could be
that had so clouded their mistress's good humour.

*   *   *

I thought over my misfortune and took heart. I carefully hid the
marks of my scourging for fear of making Eumolpus laugh at my
ill-treatment, or Giton weep over it. There was only one thing to
do to safeguard my honour, pretend to be unwell. I went to bed
and turned my blazing anger on the cause of all my disasters:

> Thrice my hand seized the dread two-edged blade,
> And thrice did he my wavering steel evade,

More soft than a cabbage-stem, swiftly too,
So what I might have, I now could not do,
For he shrank in a thousand-wrinkled fold
In fear far passing frosted winter's cold.
Nor could I coax him out, my wanted man,
But as the timid rascal baulked my plan,
To words, more wounding weapons yet, I ran.

I raised myself on my elbow, and savagely let fly at the defaulter like this: 'Well, what have you to say for yourself, you disgrace to mankind and the gods? For it would be criminal to list you among things of importance. Did I deserve your dashing me down to hell when I was seated in heaven? Your betraying the first vigour of my flowering youth, and investing me with the feebleness of decrepit old age? Well, you'd better hand me a certificate of death.'
    I vented my anger, but

> He went on looking at the ground,[16]
> His face unchanged by what I said,
> And like a drooping willow swooned
> Or slumber-weary poppy-head.

Nevertheless, when I came to the end of this horrid rebuke I began to regret all I had said, and blushed inwardly for so forgetting my self-respect as to bandy words with a part of the body that men of sterner character would certainly ignore.
    So I rubbed my forehead for some time and asked, 'But what harm have I done in ridding myself of a temper by some elementary abuse? And what about the habit of damning our guts, our bellies, and even our heads when they make us suffer too much? Eh? Didn't Ulysses squabble with his own heart? Don't some tragic heroes blast their eyes as though they could hear? Gouty sufferers curse their feet, those with chalk-stone their hands, the rheumy-eyed their eyes, and those who are always stubbing their toes derive all maladies from their feet.

> Why do you frown on me, Catos of this age,[17]
> And condemn a work of guileless innocence?
> A kind esteem smiles through my pure page,
> A homespun style reports the people's doings.
> For who does not know the act of love,

The joys of Venus? Who would forbid us
Warm our limbs in a half-warm bed?
Wise Epicurus,[18] the father of truth,
Teaches this doctrine, and says here is
The right true end of life.'

*   *   *

'Foolish prejudices are the height of insincerity in the world, and
nothing is more stupid than a false air of gravity.'

*   *   *

133 After my soliloquy I called Giton and said, 'Tell me, brother, on
your word of honour: that night Ascyltus took you from me, did
he stay awake until he had done violence to you, or was he content
with a night spent modestly on his own?'

   The boy touched his eyes and swore most precisely that Ascyltus
had not used force on him.

*   *   *

I kneeled on the threshold and spoke this prayer to the hostile god:

'Friend of the nymphs[19] and Bacchus, whom Dione in her
beauty set as god to the abundant forests, adored in Lesbos and
green Thasos, by seven-rivered Lydia, that built a temple to
you in Hypaepa: come, O master of Bacchus, safekeeper of the
Dryads' pleasure, hear my modest prayer. I do not approach
you smeared with bitter blood, nor have I raised profaning
hands against a temple, but needy and helpless I sinned, yet not
with my whole body. A man who sins through want is less
guilty. Hear my prayer, raise my heart, pardon my slight
offence; and when fortune in her hour smiles again on me, your
virtue shall not go unrewarded. To your altars shall come a
horned goat, the sire of his flock, to your altars shall come the
litter of a grunting sow, a suckling sacrifice. This year's wine
shall foam in the bowls, and drunken youth three joyful times
shall circle your shrine.'

*   *   *

As I was engaged in this prayer, keeping a careful eye on my trust, an old woman[20] came into the temple. Her hair was torn about, her clothes were black, and she was a hideous sight. She laid hands on me and drew me out by the porch.

*   *   *

'What screech-owls have gnawed at your nerves, on what cross- 134
road's dung or corpse have you trodden in the night? You could never acquit yourself even as a boy, but you were flabby, feeble, worn-out, like a hack on a hill, and wasted your labour and your sweat. And not content with sinning in your person, you have angered the gods against me!'

*   *   *

And she took me into the priestess's room again, for I offered no resistance, pushed me on the bed, seized a stick from behind the door and beat me again as I did not respond. If the stick had not splintered at the first stroke and weakened the force of her blows, she might well have broken my arms and my head. Even so I groaned at her filthy treatment, broke into a torrent of tears, covered my head with my right arm and buried myself in the pillow. The old woman was weeping too and did not know what to do, but sat on the other end of the bed and in a cracked voice began to rail at the obstacles of old age. Then the priestess came in[21] and said, 'What are you doing in my room, as though you had come to inspect a new grave? And on a holiday too, when even mourners have a smile.'

*   *   *

'Oh, Oenothea,' said the old woman, 'this young man you see here was born under an unlucky star; he cannot sell his goods to either boys or girls. You never saw anyone in such a state; he has no mainstay at all, he is not a man. The point is, what do you think of a man who left Circe's bed without tasting pleasure at all?'

When Oenothea heard this she sat down between us and shook her head for a considerable time.

'I am the only one,' she said, 'who knows how to cure this malady. Don't imagine it is any complicated affair; what I ask is that the boy should sleep with me tonight, and I will return him horn-hard:

All things on earth obey my laws. If I wish, the flower-covered
land droops and shrivels, the sap turns sluggish, and if I wish it,
she pours out wealth, and wild craggy rocks gush waters like
the very Nile. For me the sea lays down her languid waves, the
wind will shed its blast in silence before my feet. I command the
rivers and Hyrcanian tigers, and order the dragons stay still. But
these are trifling things to quote. You see the face of the moon
drawn close by incantation; Phoebus shakes, and with his
foaming steeds must turn and roll his course the other way.
Such is the power of the word. By virgin sacrifice the fire of
bulls dies and is laid, and Circe the daughter of Phoebus
changed Ulysses' men by magic chant. Proteus[22] takes what
form he pleases. I who am cunning in these arts can set the trees
of Mount Ida in the deep, or place a river on a mountain peak.'

135 A thrill of horror coursed through me at her fabulous promises, and
I started to examine the old woman more closely.

'Therefore,' cried Oenothea, 'obey my orders!'

She wiped her hands carefully, leaned over the bed, and kissed
me once, then again . . .

*   *   *

Oenothea put an old table in the middle of the altar, covered it with
live coals, and then repaired a cracked porringer, another relic of
antiquity, with warm pitch. Then she drove back into the smoke-
darkened wall a nail that she had pulled out taking down the
wooden utensil. She next put on a check apron, and set an enormous cauldron on the fire. From the meat-safe she took with a fork
a bag in which beans were stored, and bits of a hoary old brain that
had already suffered a thousand chippings. She untied the bag,
poured part of the beans on the table, and told me to shell them with
care. I obeyed her, and separated the insides from their dirty husks
with painstaking fingers. But she chided my delay, rudely gathered
up the ones I had not done, ripped the skins off with her teeth and
instantly spat them on the ground like the carcasses of flies.

*   *   *

I mused upon the ingenious shifts of poverty, the cleverness
inherent in the least detail:

No Indian ivory shone from a mount of gold, we trod no glittering marble pavement, hiding the earth that offered it, but Ceres'[23] idle grove was set round by willow hurdles, and fresh earthen pots, spun swift and crude from the potter's wheel. Then next a sweating vat, dishes of pliant osiers, pitchers stained with Bacchus' brew, and all around, a wall of clay and straw-ends, haphazard, stuck with rustic nails, from which slender rushes hung still green in the stalk. And here were low cottages with blackened beams, storing ripe sorbs wreathed in fragrant garlands, old savoury and bunches of raisins. Here was the hostess, worthy of the worship given to Hecale of old on Athenian soil. The Muse made her known to every wondering age in the years when Callimachus the poet[24] sang of her . . .

* * *

She was having a scrap of meat. As she tried to put back the brain, 136 that age-old contemporary of hers, on to the meat-hook with her fork, the rotten stool she was perched on gave way and her own weight brought the old woman down into the hearth. In so doing she broke the rim of the cauldron, put out the fire just as it was taking, burnt her elbow on an ember, and got her face covered all over with the ashes she raised. I started up and set the old woman on her feet, but not without a laugh. And at once she rushed out to the neighbours for something to repair the fire with, so as not to retard the sacrifice in any way.

I went to the door of the place. But here were the three sacred geese! I suppose they habitually arrived at midday for their commons from the old woman. At any rate, they charged and surrounded me as I trembled at their hideous, insane cackling. One of them tore my clothes, another undid my shoestrings and drew them out; the third, king and commander of the barbarians, simply set about my leg with his saw-edged bill. I was not amused. I wrenched a leg off the table and with this weapon in my hand started cudgelling my obstreperous webfoot. I did not stop at one perfunctory blow. I wreaked my vengeance by laying the goose dead.

I think the birds of Stymphalus fled this way sky-high when Hercules compelled them; like the Harpies[25] with their dripping wings when they wet with poison the tantalising feast laid out

for Phineus. The upper air reverberated, and sobbed as never
before; the Celestial Court was confounded . . .

*   *   *

By now the survivors had picked up the beans that had spilled and
rolled over the floor, and I imagined they had returned to the temple
after the loss of their leader. I was doubly pleased, with my prize and
my revenge, and dumped the slaughtered goose behind the bed. I
bathed my leg-wound, which was not deep, with vinegar. Then I
thought out a way of escape, as I was afraid of trouble. I got my
things together and started from the house. I had scarcely put my
foot over the doorstep of the room when I saw Oenothea coming
with a crock full of burning coals. I recoiled, threw off my coat, and
stood there in the entrance as though impatiently expecting her.
Kindling the fire with some broken reeds, she added wood, and
apologised for being late; a woman she knew had not let her leave
without draining the three customary cups.

'And what have you been doing while I was out?' she asked.
'Where are my beans?'

Well, thinking I had brought off something praiseworthy, I fought
the battle again for her blow by blow, and to put an end to her misery
I offered the goose by way of compensation. When the old woman
saw it, she raised such a shriek it was like another gaggle of geese
coming in the door. Deafened by the noise, and wondering what
bizarre crime I had committed, I asked the reason for her flaring up
and why she was more upset about the goose than me.

137   But she clapped her hands together: 'Oh, you villain, to dare
open your mouth! Do you mean to say you don't realise the
enormity of the sin you have committed? You have killed the pet
of Priapus, the goose all our women are mad about. So don't
pretend you've done nothing. If the magistrates get to know you'll
be crucified. You have defiled my home with blood, and until now
it has been unspotted, and any of my enemies can deprive me of
my priesthood if he wants to because of what you have done.'

*   *   *

'Please don't make so much noise,' I said, 'I'll give you an ostrich
in place of your goose.'

*   *   *

To my astonishment she sat down on the bed and wept for the death of her goose. In the meantime Proselenus came in with purchases for the sacrifice. Seeing a dead bird she wanted to know why we were down at heart, and on hearing why began to shed hot tears at my misfortune, as though I had killed my own father and not a common goose.

I was out of all patience with this mummery, and said, 'Look here, can I cleanse my hands of this with money? Even supposing I had insulted you, or done murder? Here are two gold pieces.[26] With these you can bribe the gods and buy geese as well.'

When she saw them Oenothea said, 'Forgive me, young man, but I am only anxious for your sake. It is a proof of love and not of spite. We will take care that nobody finds out. Just pray to the gods and ask them to pardon your misdeed.'

> The man with money always sails with the wind,
> And trims his fortune freely.
> If he wanted he could marry Danaë even,
> And make Acrisius believe what he told her.
> If he were poet or public speaker,
> He would rattle them all;
> He out Catos Cato and wins his case.
> Imagine him lawyer; he imposes
> 'Proven' and 'Not proven',
> Servius and Labco[27] rolled into one.
> To say no more: with money at hand,
> You make a wish, and what you want will come.
> Jupiter is encaged by the sides of your strong-box.

She placed a bowl of wine under my hands, made me spread my fingers out wide, and cleansed them with leeks and parsley. Then, muttering some formula, she threw filberts into the wine. And as they sank or swam, so she prognosticated. But I was not unaware that the hollow nuts, those filled with air and without kernels, would float on the surface, and that the weight of the ripe and solid ones would sink them to the bottom.

*   *   *

She laid the bird open, drew out an abnormally fat liver, and told me the future from it. She went even further in covering the traces

of my crime; she carved up the whole goose, and produced an
exquisite roast for one who a moment ago, she said, was doomed
to die. And with it went a good strong wine.

*   *   *

138 Oenothea got out a leather phallus which she covered in oil,
ground pepper, and crushed nettle-seed, and pushed it up me little
by little. The unfeeling old woman next anointed my thighs . . .

*   *   *

She mixed the juice of nasturtiums with southernwood and bathed
my parts with it, and seizing a bunch of green nettles began to beat
gently all that lay below the navel.

*   *   *

Giddy with wine and passion though they were, the old hags tried
to take the same route, and followed their runaway through a
number of streets, crying 'Stop thief!' But I got away, with my toes
all bloody from my headlong flight.

*   *   *

'Chrysis, who loathed your old ways, intends to take up with your
new ones, even at the risk of her neck.'

*   *   *

'Ariadne or Leda,[28] had they any beauty like this? What had Helen or
Venus to compare with it? Paris himself, judge to the contending
goddesses, if Paris had seen her, if his wanton eyes had seen and
compared her, he would have sacrificed for her Helen and all the
goddesses. If only I might steal a kiss, or clasp her heavenly, godlike
breast, perhaps my body would regain its vigour, and those parts
dulled, as I think, by a drug would come into their own again. No
outrage shall dismay me. Have I been beaten up? Think nothing of it!
Thrown out? A joke, of course. If only I might rekindle her favour!'

*   *   *

139 I harrowed my bed, handling it over and over as if I held the image
of my love.

*   *   *

Implacable fate and the gods do not pursue me alone. There was Hercules, who, driven from the Argive shore, bore the weight of the heavens. Laomedon before me sated the outraged anger of the gods. Pelias felt Juno's wrath, Telephus bore arms in ignorance, and Ulysses quaked in Neptune's kingdom. And I, on land or hoary Nereus' seas,[29] am followed by the heavy wrath of Priapus of the Hellespont.

✳   ✳   ✳

I asked my Giton if anybody had called for me.

'Nobody today,' he said. 'But yesterday a woman came in,[30] fairly good-looking, and when she had worn me down with an interminable conversation and endless questions, she finally told me you deserved to be punished like a slave, and would be if the injured party upheld his complaint.'

*   *   *

I had not finished my lament when Chrysis came in and threw herself upon me with fierce embraces.

'Now,' she said, 'I have you as I hoped to find you. My desire, my love! My flame shall never die unless you quench it in your blood.'

*   *   *

Suddenly one of the new servants came running up and confirmed that our master was most furious[31] that I had been off duty for two days. And it would be as well for me to have ready some suitable excuse; it seemed hardly possible that his rage would subside without a beating.

*   *   *

One of the most respectable of women, Philomela by name, who had extorted many a legacy in her day, was now old and had lost her good looks. She continued her practice vicariously by introducing her son and daughter among the aged and childless. So she came to Eumolpus with her children to entrust them to his wisdom and commendable goodness . . . she confided her wishes in him. He was the only person in the whole world who could daily give sound advice to the young. In short, she would leave her children in Eumolpus's house to hear his discourse, the one legacy that could be imparted to youth. She was as good as her word. She left a most ravishing daughter and her young brother in his room, and made a pretext of going to the temple to name him in her prayers. Eumolpus, so chaste a man that even I appeared a likely lad to him, lost no time in inviting the girl to make a sacrifice to Venus Callipyge.[32] But as he had put it about that he had gout and weak loins, he saw that unless he kept up his act there would be some danger of ruining the whole imposture. So to give credence to his lie, he begged the girl to squat on the advantage he had to offer, and ordered Corax to slide beneath the bed he lay on, lean his hands on the floor and heave him with his back. Corax obeyed with cool deliberation, and stroke for stroke alternated with the girl's technique. When the exercise was nearing its end, Eumolpus raised his voice to encourage Corax to put all he had into it. Thus the old man, between his hireling and his lass, seemed to be playing at swings. Eumolpus did it twice over, to our great mirth, and his too. As for me, not to let a lusty chance slip idly by, seeing the brother admire his sister's gymnastics through a crack, I came up to see if he would submit to like damage. The knowledgeable boy did not scorn my embraces, but here too I came up against my hostile deity.[33]

*   *   *

'It is the more influential gods who have restored me whole. Surely Mercury himself, who leads souls across and brings them back again, has by his own goodwill returned to me what an angry hand cut off. You will see that I have been more handsomely endowed than Protesilaus was or any other of the ancients.'

With this I lifted my shirt, and got Eumolpus's wholehearted approval. Although at first he curled up in terror, and then, the better to believe his eyes, grasped in both hands the gift of the gods.

*   *   *

'Socrates, beloved of men and gods,[34] boasted that he never looked into a shop nor stayed to watch any large gathering. You see that nothing is more fitting than to constantly commune with philosophy.'

'This is all quite true,' I said, 'nor is it less true that no man more

deserves to be dashed down by ill-fortune than one of those who
lust after another's goods. How else could rogues and pickpockets
live, without purses jingling with money to throw for bait among
the crowd? Just as dumb animals are drawn to morsels, so men
would never be taken but in the hope of something to bite on.'

*   *   *

'The ship you promised from Africa[35] with your money and your   141
household has not put in to port. The legacy-hunters are drained
dry and have curtailed their generosity. Unless I'm mistaken,
Fortune, our general mistress, begins to repent of her favours.'

*   *   *

'All who have legacies under my will, apart from my freedmen, get
them on this condition – that they cut my body to pieces and eat it
in public.'[36]

*   *   *

'We do know that among certain nations a law is still observed that
requires the next-of-kin to eat their dead, and to the extent that the
sick are often upbraided for spoiling the flesh they will leave. In
saying this, I would remind my friends not to run counter to my
wishes; in the same spirit as they damn my soul they must devour
my body.'

*   *   *

The inordinate fame of his wealth clouded the eyes and minds of
these wretches.

*   *   *

Gorgias was ready to go through with it.

*   *   *

'I am not perturbed by your belly's revolting. It will obey your
command if for one hour of nausea you promise it a recompense of
countless good things. Simply close your eyes, and imagine you are
eating, not human flesh, but hundreds of thousands in money. In
addition we shall devise a number of seasonings that will change
the taste. For no meat is pleasant by itself; its nature is changed by

art, and it is reconciled to a reactionary stomach. If you need examples to recommend my plan, the Saguntines ate human flesh when besieged by Hannibal, and they had nothing to live for. The Petilians did the same in the extremes of famine, and they sought nothing from this banquet except to appease their hunger. When Numantia was taken by Scipio they found mothers with the half-eaten bodies of their children clutched to the breast.'

DESUNT CETERA

FRAGMENTS

1

Servius on Virgil, *Aeneid* III, 57: *auri sacra fames.* Here *sacra* means cursed, a word originating in a Gallic custom. Whenever the Massilians endured a plague, one of their paupers would present himself to be fed for a whole year, at public expense, on ritually purified food. He would then be arrayed in sacred greenery and garments, and curses heaped on his head while he was conducted all round the city. Thus he would be burdened with all the ills of the colony, and so he would be banished. All this can be read in Petronius.

2

Servius on Virgil, *Aeneid*, XIII, 159, on nouns of the feminine gender ending in *-tor.* However, if the nouns do not derive from a verb, they are of common gender, both masculine and feminine having a similar ending in *-tor*, as in a male or female *senator*, or a male or female *balneator* [bath attendant]. Even so, Petronius permits himself the form *balneatrix*.

3

Pseudo-Acron on Horace, *Epodes* 5, 48: *Canidia rodens pollicem.* He describes the stance and emotions of Canidia in a temper. Petronius, pointing out someone in a rage, says, 'biting his thumb to the raw'.

4

Sidonius Apollinaris, *Carmina* 23:

145   How may I commend you,
             Masters of Latin eloquence?
             Poets of Arpinum,
             Padua and Mantua?

155   And you, O Arbiter,
             Equal of Hellespontine Priapus,
             Worshipper of the sacred tree-trunk,
             Settler in the gardens of Massilia.

5

Priscianus, *Institutiones* 8, 16 and 11, 29, Hertz (ed.): giving examples of past participles of deponent verbs with passive meanings, says Petronius has 'the soul encompassed in our breast'.

6

Boethius, on Porphyry's *Isagoge*, translated by Victorinus: 'I shall do that with the greatest pleasure,' I said. 'But since, as Petronius phrases it, "the morning sun has smiled favourably on the rooftops", let us rise, and if there is anything in the matter in hand, deal with it more attentively later on.'

7

Fulgentius, *Mitologiarum* I, 23: you may not know . . . how much women abhor satire. Before the flood-tide of a woman's words advocates give way, literati cannot put two words together, a spokesman is silent and the crier refrains from his utterance – but then satire is the only way to restrain their madness, although Albucia in Petronius is a case in point . . .

8

Fulgentius, *Mitologiarum* III, 8, p. 124, where he points out that essence of myrrh is extremely strong: Here too Petronius says he took a cup of myrrh to excite his lust.

9

Fulgentius, in his account of the contents of Virgil, p. 156: We have in fact already disclosed the relevance of the fable of three-headed Cerberus to the squabbles and lawsuits of the courts. Petronius says of Euscion, 'he was a Cerberus at the bar'.

10

Fulgentius, *Sermonum Antiquorum* 42, p. 565: *ferculum* means a platter of meat. So Petronius Arbiter says, 'after the platter was brought in'.

11

Fulgentius, *ibid.* 46, p. 565: *valgia* is in fact the contortion of the lips while vomiting. Petronius says, 'with his lips twisted as when throwing up'.

12

Fulgentius, *ibid.* p. 566: *alucinare* means to dream idly, and comes from *alucitae*, which we call *conopes,* mosquitoes. Petronius Arbiter says, 'the mosquitoes were annoying my companion'.

13

Fulgentius, *ibid.* 60, p. 567: *manubiae* means the ornaments of kings. So Petronius says, 'so many regal ornaments found in the hands of a fugitive'.

14

Fulgentius, *ibid.* 61, p. 567: *aumatium* is a private spy-hole, as at a public theatre or circus. So Petronius says, 'I flung myself into the spy-hole'.

15

Isodorus, *Originum* V, 26, 7: *dolus* (trickery) describes the cunning mind of someone who deceives, feigning one thing and doing another. Petronius differs when he says, 'What, members of the jury, is *dolus*? It is without doubt an act that violates the law (*quod legi dolet*). There you have *dolum*, now for *malum* . . . '

16

Glossary of St Dionysius: a springboard (*petaurus*) refers to the realm of sport. Petronius says, 'rising up high as the springboard demanded'.

17

Glossary of St Dionysius: Petronius has, 'It was sufficiently clear that unless they bent double they would never pass through the underground passage at Naples.'

18

Nicolaus Perottus, *Cornu copiae* (1513), p. 200: Cosmus was indeed an excellent maker of unguents, and ointments were named Cosmian after him. Juvenal 8, 86 also has, 'even when completely immersed in a bronze Cosmian jar'. Petronius: 'He said, bring us an alabaster casket of Cosmian.'

19

Terentianus Maurus, *On Metre*:

> We see Horace
> Nowhere using
> Verses of this metre
> Persistently,
> Yet the eloquent
> Arbiter piles them up,
> In his works.
> You may recall
> How we sang
> 'Maids of Memphis
> Made ready for rites
> Of the Gods.
> A boy black as night
> Gesticulates.'

Marius Victorinus III, 17: We know that some lyric poets introduced certain verses of this form and metre in their poems, and we find this in the Arbiter as well, e.g.

> Maids of Memphis
> Made ready for rites
> Of the Gods

and

> Black as night
> Egyptian choruses.

20

Terentius Maurus, *On Metre*, VI, p. 409: The division we now speak of reveals the metre used, they say, by Anacreon when he composed his delightful songs. We find Petronius and many another using it, when he says that this lyric poet sang words conforming to the Muses. But I will show what caesura occurs in this verse – *iuverunt segetes meum laborem* (the cornfields made light work of my labour), *iuverunt* being the beginning of this hexameter. The rest of the words – *segetes meum laborem* – are the same as *triplici vides ut ortu*:

> You see the lustre of the moon
> Revolve in three risings,
> And Phoebus' wingèd wheel
> Crosses the scurrying globe.

21

Diomedes, *On Grammar*, III: From this comes the caesura which the Arbiter uses in:

> An old wine-sodden woman
> Her lips all aquiver.

22

Servius, *On the Grammar of Donatus*: He also uses *Quirites* only as a plural, although we read in Horace *hunc Quiritem* (this Roman citizen), so that there is a nominative, *Quiris*, such as Petronius uses.

Pompeius in his *Commentary on the Art of Donatus*: No one says *hic Quiretes* (this citizen), but instead *hi Quiretes* (these citizens),

although you might read the former usage. Reading Petronius you
will find the nominative singular an established fact: *hic Quiretes* is
what he says.

23

A grammarian on nouns of uncertain gender. Fretum (a strait) is neuter,
its plural is *freta*; Petronius uses *freta Nereidum* (the sea-straits of the
Nereids).

24

Jerome, *Epistle to Demetriades* 130, 19: Boys with tight-curled and
crimped hair, with skins smelling like alien muskrats, of whom the
Arbiter wrote, 'he does not smell well who always gives off a good
odour' – a warning to the virgin to avoid them, and other scourges
of modesty, like the plague.

25

Fulgentius, *Mitologiarum* II, 6 (Helm on Prometheus): Although
Nicagoras . . . notes that Prometheus was the first to project the
image that depicts the vulture exposing the liver as if it were the
personification of spite. Hence Petronius Arbiter says

> The vulture that pierces through
> Our deep liver to extract
> The heart and hidden nerves
> Is no cordial bird, as poets say,
> But envy and excess, a vileness
> Of heart.

26

> When the raven lays eggs as corn is ripening,
> She contradicts Nature's old and tested ways.
> The procreant bear licks cubs into shape;
> Fish starved of love's embrace are apt to spawn;
> Apollo's tortoise, released from parental care,
> Will hatch eggs by her own nostrils' warmth.
> The solitary bee, roused from its waxen cell,
> Stocks the encampment with zealous militia.
> Nature's strength, then, lies not in one strict way,
> But in the pleasures of mutability.

27

In this world, fear first created gods,
And lightning fell from the heavens.
Ramparts collapsed in flame.
Athos was struck and blazed with fire.
Phoebus sank behind the earth he rolled around,
The moon grew old, then revived her glory.
Constellations were strewn across the world,
The year divided into differing months.
Such lunacy persisted; worthless delusion
Compelled farmers to offer Ceres
First fruits, to wreathe Bacchus with garlands,
And made Pales exult in the shepherds' toil.
Neptune lays claim to the world's waters
As they submerge him, and Pallas
To the huts and hostelries. And one whose
Prayer has been answered, or who
Has turned the world to profit
Now lies in greedy competition
To fashion his own Gods.

28

There are men who would sooner eat fire
Than safeguard a secret. Whatever chatter
Springs from your front porch will rebound
Off the city walls like urgent rumour.
Such broken trust does not end there;
Betrayal's an act that aggravates
The scandal. When that slave, bursting
To break the news, dug a hole in the ground
And deposited the tale of the king's ass's ears,
The earth first let out murmurings
And then babbling reeds betrayed Midas,
Just as the informer had spread it abroad.

29

Our eyes deceive us. Our senses
Stray and trouble the mind, and

Lie to us. This tower hard by is square;
From a distance its corners are round.
A well-gorged belly spurns even
Hybla's honey, and time and again
Cassia offends the nostrils.
So this or that might never
Please or displease, unless the senses
Were forever compelled to lock in strife,
To battle with doubt, trembling in the balance.

30

Dreams that mock the mind
With flitting shadows,
The powers do not send these down
From heaven nor from some fastness
Of the gods. No, each man
Makes his own. When repose
Enfolds our limbs laid low with sleep,
Our featherweight minds are in brisk pursuit
By night of what was thought by day.
He who shatters towns in war and destroys
Cities with harrowing flame imagines
Missiles and routed armies,
The death of kings, and battlefields
Flowing over with blood. Lawyers conceive
Not the case they plead but statutes
And courtrooms, while in horror they see
The bench secured by guards.
The skinflint buries his treasure,
Then stumbles on surfaced gold.
A huntsman rends the woodlands
With his pack of hounds; a drowning sailor
Plucked overboard rights the keel
Of his boat; this mistress writes
A love-letter, that adulteress sends
A gift, and the dog sleeps on and marks
The footing of the hare.
In the tarrying of the night
The wounds of the hapless abide.

NOTES

In preparing these notes, which I have kept to a minimum, I had in mind a general audience, which would not be entirely unfamiliar with ancient Greek and Roman civilisation. So, for example, I have refrained from explaining who Homer, Virgil, or Hercules were. My main concern has been to provide not scholarly comments, but explanatory notes which would enable the reader of this fragmentary text to follow the plot and to understand jokes or allusions which have now become unintelligible to the general reader.

CHAPTER ONE

1 1 **The adventures at the school of rhetoric and at the brothel.** The division of the *Satyricon* into chapters, and the chapter headings, do not appear in the manuscripts of the novel. The latter are my additions to Petronius' text in order to indicate to the reader the episodic structure of the novel's narrative, and to enable him or her to follow the complicated plot more easily.

2 **'But are they not the same Furies that torment our public speakers?** The opening scene of the surviving sections of the novel depicts the narrator Encolpius, in the colonnade of a school of rhetoric, declaiming vehemently against the educational system of his time.

3 **Sophocles and Euripides.** Two of the three great tragic playwrights in fifth century BC Athens. Aeschylus is, perhaps deliberately, missing from Encolpius' list.

4 **Pindar and the nine lyric poets.** According to one tradition, these were Alcaeus, Alcmaeon, Anacreon, Arion, Bacchylides, Ibycus, Sappho, Simonides, and Stesichorus. The renowned Theban lyric poet Pindar, here mentioned separately, should conventionally count as one of the nine.

5 **neither Plato nor Demosthenes**. The former was a philosopher, the latter a statesman and an orator; both were great prose-writers in fourth century BC Athens.

6 **wind-filled blabbering**. Encolpius refers to the pompous and turgid Asiatic (in contrast to the pure Attic) style of oratory. By Neronian times, however, this rhetorical debate was hardly controversial.

7 **Thucydides or Hyperides?** The great fifth-century BC historian recounted, in a superbly precise style of writing, the growth and fall of the Athenian empire in his *Peloponnesian War*. The rhetorical skill of Hyperides, a fourth-century BC Athenian orator, was considered second only to that of Demosthenes.

8 **Lucilius**. A Campanian cavalryman (*eques*, the second highest social class in Rome) of the second century BC, regarded as the inventor of the literary genre of Roman satire (in the modern sense of the word). The Augustan poet Horace, who was greatly influenced by him, refers to his impressive speed of composition.

9 **Sirens**. Greek mythological birds with women's faces. By their beautiful song they led sailors to destruction on the coast of Southern Italy.

10 **Everybody, everywhere, . . . we repulsed the troublemaker**. Presumably Encolpius and Ascyltus are still in the brothel.

11 **I asked my brother**. The term 'brother', used here of Giton and later of both Ascyltus and Encolpius, means 'lover'.

12 **'If you're Lucretia, . . . you've met your Tarquin.'** Lucretia, wife of L. Tarquinius Collatinus and an exemplar of female chastity and marital loyalty, committed suicide after she was raped by the king Tarquinius Superbus' lustful son Sextus Tarquinius.

13 **'Shut up, you filthy cut-throat!'** Although committing murder, participating in a gladiatorial show, and partaking in a sexual incident in a garden are actions not incompatible with Encolpius' character, there is not enough evidence to prove that these are real facts of Encolpius' past, recounted in missing sections of the text.

CHAPTER TWO

1 **our stolen cloak**. It becomes apparent from the surviving text that
   in a previous (now lost) section of the novel, set in the country-
   side, the heroes stole a rustic's expensive cloak and lost a shirt with
   stolen money in it.

2 **fate had cleared me of the worst suspicions**. Encolpius must
   have been either openly accused or suspected of keeping the stolen
   gold for himself.

3 **with the Cynic's scrip**. The Cynic philosophers, originally a
   fourth century BC sect, of whom the best known was Diogenes,
   regarded luxury with scorn on the grounds that money was
   incompatible with the superior life of the philosopher.

4 **A ready-made win is never a pleasure**. The ending of this story
   does not survive. Encolpius' parenthetical statement, 'We had got
   back our savings, *or so we thought*', suggests either that the money
   was not in the shirt after all or that the heroes had to give it to
   somebody.

5 **whose rite you interrupted by the grotto**. Presumably this is a
   reference to the secret, women-only rites in honour of Priapus,
   the phallic god of fertility, who seems to be pursuing Encolpius as
   Poseidon had pursued Odysseus. Quartilla herself will also refer, in
   her ensuing monologue, to the 'intrusion' of Encolpius and his
   friends in the shrine of Priapus; nevertheless, her words are too
   vague to allow a detailed reconstruction of the missing episode.

6 Although the text is extremely fragmentary here, and contains
   events which will be repeated later in the same episode (e.g. the
   appearance of the catamite), the plot is fairly clear and the ritual
   elements of this orgy are obvious (e.g. tying of hands and feet,
   smearing the face with soot), though not easy to explain.

7 **Falernian wine**. See note 15 on p. 137.

8 **Don't you know that our sleeper means just that?** In the Latin
   text Quartilla plays with the double sense of the noun *embasicoetas*,
   a Greek word meaning both a drinking mug (presumably of
   obscene shape) and a sodomite.

CHAPTER THREE

1 **the third day. A free-for-all banquet . . . the storm to come.**
   Due to the gap in the manuscripts the reference to 'the third day'
   cannot be explained with certainty. Might it be the third day after
   Encolpius received the invitation to a free meal? Or, more likely,
   is it the third day since Encolpius and company encountered
   Quartilla for the second time? In any case, this allusion, marking
   conventionally the beginning of a new episode in the life of
   Encolpius, is linked with the equally enigmatic reference to 'a
   free-for-all banquet', nowadays interpreted as the dinner supplied
   free to gladiators on the eve of a fatal contest. The beginning of the
   next sentence (**But . . .**) implies that this banquet would not be
   disagreeable to Encolpius, so it is unlikely that it is a meal provided
   by Quartilla; on the other hand, it is surely not Trimalchio's feast,
   for it has not been mentioned yet, and when it is mentioned, it fills
   Encolpius with joy rather than trepidation. Perhaps this expression
   is used metaphorically to denote a forthcoming nasty incident,
   which the heroes were afraid of, and which has nothing to do with
   Quartilla; the same incident may be meant by the vague phrase
   'how to avoid the storm to come'.

2 **Trimalchio.** Generally taken as a name of Semitic origin, meaning
   'Thrice-wealthy' or 'Thrice-lord' .

3 **a clock in his dining-room . . . a trumpeter.** Neither an actual
   clock nor a trumpeter reappear in the text as we have it; the horn-
   trumpet mentioned in the text was conventionally used by sailors to
   announce their arrival at a port, by oxherds and swineherds to gather
   their herds together, and by the Roman army to mark the night-
   watches or to summon and give orders to the soldiers. Its use by
   Trimalchio, therefore, to announce the passing of time, displays his
   spectacular eccentricity together with his vulgar superstition, examples of which will occur repeatedly before and during the feast.

4 **in a red shirt.** Red indicated wealth and social importance, but
   was certainly not a respectable colour for an old man; nevertheless,
   it was perfect for Trimalchio's effeminate extravagance.
   Trimalchio's tunic is only a slight hint of the tasteless multi-
   coloured costumes which he himself, his wife and his household
   will be wearing throughout this episode.

5 **long-haired boys.** A sign of effeminacy; this aside comment
   discloses the homoerotic desires of both Encolpius and Trimalchio

6 **Menelaus**. See note 2 on p. 144.

7 **Falernian**. See note 15 on p. 137.

8 **a wizened, blear-eyed boy**. Croesus, a name probably chosen for its connotations of wealth (he will reappear on p. 46). Trimalchio himself had once been a pet-slave; now he in turn is in a position to have his own pet-slave.

9 **Mercury's staff . . . Minerva**. The presence of the god of commerce and the goddess of wisdom indicates to the visitor that Trimalchio is successful both as a businessman and as an intellectual.

10 **the beard of the great man himself**. The cutting of the beard for the first time symbolised the passage from boyhood to manhood, and keeping it was not an uncommon phenomenon; so this passage need not be regarded as evidence that Trimalchio is a caricature of Nero, who did keep his first beard in a gold box.

11 **a show by Laenas' gladiators**. Encolpius' reference to a picture of gladiators in action (sponsored by Laenas, an otherwise unknown magistrate) next to scenes from the Homeric classics exemplifies Trimalchio's vulgar taste; imagine today the effect of having a Rembrandt next to a poster of a third-division football team.

12 **Priest of Augustus' College**. Trimalchio (as well as one of his guests, Habinnas) was a member of a religious board consisting of commissioners, whose task was to ensure that the rites in honour of the deified Augustus were carried out properly.

13 **real Tyrian purple**. The boastful remark of the treasurer on the high cost of his clothes is meant to echo Trimalchio's haughtiness and arrogance.

14 **Trimalchio himself was brought in**. After two unforgettable appearances at the playground and at the baths, Trimalchio enters the dining-room dressed in a manner which constitutes the climax of his extravagance. His vulgar luxury is indicated by his effeminacy ('diminutive cushions', 'scarlet cloak'), his desire to show off his wealth ('he bared his right arm to reveal a gold armlet and a circle of ivory clasped by a lustrous flat piece of metal'), his superstition ('[his ring] was entirely composed of star-like points of steel'), and his pretence to belong to an important social class ('a napkin with a nobleman's purple stripe', 'a huge gilded ring').

15 **Falernian**. This was highly esteemed wine of Campanian origin, but the point of the joke is that the wine was not bottled as early as

Opimius' consulship (121 BC). Trimalchio is cheating to impress
his guests.

16 **a silver skeleton**. The spectacle of the skeleton is a trivial example
of the *memento mori* motif, which was frequently employed at
dinners to remind guests that life was short and fragile: consequently, they should enjoy it as much as possible The silver
material of the skeleton and the improvised show Trimalchio
performs using the skeleton as a prop are, of course, signs of his
vulgar taste.

17 **a round plate with the twelve signs of the Zodiac**. The
connection between each star-sign and the items of food on the
zodiac dish is not always clear, and includes similarity in shape,
sophisticated astrological reasons and mere childish word-play.

18 **The Laserwort Seller**. This passage is our only piece of evidence
for the existence of such a title among the surviving fragments of
the Roman mime. We know nothing of the popularity or the plot
of this mime, which may be important for the proper understanding
of the Petronian context.

19 **Pegasus . . . Marsyas**. Pegasus was the famous winged horse of
Greek mythology, which sprang from the blood of the Gorgon
Medusa when Perseus decapitated her. Marsyas is the Greek satyr
who challenged Apollo to a music competition. He played on the
flute and Apollo on the lyre; he lost and was flayed alive by the god.

20 **'Carve 'er, carver'**. The pun is better in Latin, where the vocative
case of Carpus' name and the imperative mood of the verb used by
Trimalchio to order his slave are one and the same – *carpe*.

21 **he snatched the cap off a gnome, and unearthed a treasure-
hoard**. A peculiar proverbial saying which seems to have
originated from the fairytale belief in the existence of a capped
goblin who guarded treasure; if one stole its cap, one would also
get the treasure.

22 **Is this what Ulysses means to you?** This was the warning of the
priest Laocoon to the optimistic Trojans not to believe so readily
that the Greeks, having failed to capture Troy, had really departed
leaving behind them the Trojan horse. Thus Trimalchio wants
both to show off that he knows his Virgil (*Aeneid* II, 44), and to
equate himself with the cunning Odysseus. Odysseus was a
trickster in military affairs, but Trimalchio seems to be cunning
only in culinary ones.

23 **Hipparchus and Aratus**. Hipparchus was a celebrated second century BC astronomer from Nicaea. He wrote a commentary on the astronomical work of Aratus (third century BC) entitled *Phaenomena*, a poem translated by Cicero and not altogether free from scientific errors. The whole passage should be interpreted as an ironical comment of the narrator.

24 '**Dionysus . . . be thou free.**' . . . '**You won't deny that I have a father who makes free.**' This apparently silly joke is a complicated and untranslatable word-play on Dionysus (the name of Trimalchio's slave and of a Greek god) and the Latin words *liber* (= free), *Liber* (Roman god of vegetation, identified with the Greek god Dionysus), *pater liber* (= a free father; no freedman had a free father), *Pater Liber* (the standard Roman title for the god Dionysus), and *habere* (= to have, but also 'to possess as a master').

25 **you could safely play guess-how-many-fingers with him in the dark**. This game must have involved two players at a time; one would put his hand behind his back and raise some fingers, while the other guessed the correct number of fingers. The game is mentioned here surely to illustrate the trustworthiness and reliability of Safinius' character, rather than, as some have suggested, his outstanding ability to win this game in the dark.

26 **as the yokel said when he lost his brindled pig**. Might that be a character from a popular farcical sketch?

27 **Their barker said**. The task of this slave is rather strange, if we take into account that his usual duty was to remind his forgetful master of people's names.

28 **it borders on Tarracina and Tarentum**. Tarracina is in Latium, Tarentum in Southern Italy.

29 **controversy**. A technical term in schools of rhetoric, indicating a type of formal debate, usually on a far-fetched legal theme, in which the adversaries were required to deliver speeches for the prosecution and the defence.

30 **and how the Cyclops twisted his thumb with the tongs**. Some scholars are unwilling to interpret this story as yet another example of Trimalchio's amusingly confused erudition, but trace its origin to a now lost literary incident, in which the Cyclops cut Ulysses' thumb to stop him using the oars of a boat, and so leaving the monster's island.

31 **I saw her hanging in a bottle at Cumae.** The Cumaean Sibyl was a prophetess, who gained immortality but not eternal youth; through age she shrank so much that she was able to fit inside a bottle, and yearned to die. She appears in Virgil, not in Homer, as Trimalchio implies.

32 **When Ilium fell, Hannibal.** The formidable Carthaginian leader was not, of course, associated with the conquest of either Troy or Corinth, but with Saguntum (219 BC), whose inhabitants voluntarily destroyed their possessions to prevent Hannibal from acquiring them.

33 **how Cassandra killed her children . . . Daedalus shuts Niobe in the Trojan horse . . . Hermeros and Petraites.** Wonderfully Trimalchionesque 'spoof' of Greek mythology. It was Medea who killed her children to punish Jason for marrying another woman; the prophetess Cassandra was Priam's daughter, fated to be disbelieved by everyone and eventually killed by Agamemnon's wife. Daedalus was the architect of the famous Cretan Labyrinth, the abode of the carnivorous Minotaur, who was the offspring of king Minos' wife Pasiphae and a bull. In order to copulate with the animal, she got inside a wooden image of a cow, constructed by Daedalus. Niobe was the mother of seven sons and seven daughters, all of whom were slain by Leto's two children, Apollo and Artemis. The wooden Trojan horse, filled with soldiers, was the means by which the Greeks managed to enter, and finally destroy, Troy. Hermeros and Petraites were famous first century AD gladiators. Mugs with pop singers or footballers on them would be the modern equivalent of Trimalchio's precious cups.

34 **cordax.** A lascivious dance originally associated with the Greek farcical stage.

35 **Medeia perimadeia!** So far there has not been scholarly agreement about the precise meaning or the origin of the words (if, indeed, this is the correct reading in the manuscripts) which the slaves sang in chorus to accompany Trimalchio's gestures.

36 **the name of a major domo banished to Baiae.** This is hardly a severe punishment, since Baiae was a fashionable resort for wealthy aristocrats situated in the Bay of Naples; however, the porter's banishment demonstrates Trimalchio's pretensions to imperial power.

37 **Mopsus of Thrace.** Is Trimalchio thinking here of the singer

Orpheus of Thrace? As it stands, the text does not make sense, and perhaps is not intended to do so.

38 **Publilius**. A famous first century BC Syrian writer and performer of farcical mimes, which contained moral apophthegms. It is very tempting to dismiss Trimalchio's unexpected comparison between Cicero and Publilius as yet another pseudo-intellectual whim of the semi-educated host. Note that, though Trimalchio invites his guests to express an opinion on this issue, he does not really allow them to do so, and also that he passes very quickly from one topic of conversation to the other without really discussing anything in depth.

39 **When did you pay off your five per cent for freedom?** Mid-December was the time of the *Saturnalia*, the winter-festival in honour of Saturn, the god of agriculture; during this period slaves were allowed freedom to revel together with free men. Every time a slave was manumitted, a fee was due to the public treasury; this amounted to five per cent of the slave's value (see p. 47, '[Scissa] will have an exorbitant sum to pay in manumission dues; they value the deceased at fifty thousand'). With these two remarks, therefore, the angry speaker Hermeros implies that Giton is behaving inappropriately.

40 **the Homeric actors**. These performers, not to be confused with rhapsodists, were low-class declaimers of Homeric themes, who appeared in theatres and used cheap but impressive tricks in their performances, such as retractable daggers or false blood. It is unclear whether Trimalchio owns this troupe of actors or has hired their services only for the night.

41 **Do you know what story they're doing?** Another splendidly confused account of Greek mythology. The theme seems to be the war between the Greeks and the Trojans (not the Parentines, as Trimalchio says). Diomede was a brave Greek hero in the Trojan war; Ganymede was not a relative of Diomede, but the beautiful Trojan youth who was kidnapped by Zeus and became the god's cup-bearer in Olympus; the beautiful Helen of Troy, wife of king Menelaus of Sparta, was the sister of the twins Castor and Pollux, not of Ganymede and Diomede. She was abducted by the Trojan prince Paris and not by Agamemnon, who was Menelaus' brother and a great general involved in the Greek expedition against Troy; he had to sacrifice his daughter Iphigenia in order to gain favourable winds for the Greek ships to sail from Aulis; Iphigenia was told to

go to Aulis to marry the Greek hero Achilles; in fact, she neither married nor died there, for Diana substituted a deer in her place and took her as her priestess. During the war Achilles was slain by Paris. When his armour was awarded to Odysseus, Ajax, another Greek warrior, went mad out of envy. The story of Ajax is the last detail in this mythological hotch-potch, because Trimalchio is using it to pave the way for the next course.

42 **Lares**. The household gods. Trimalchio has such a high opinion of himself that he has included his own image amongst the statuettes of the *Lares*.

43 **Thus he spake**. The old-fashioned style of translation here suits the formulaic expression of the Latin text, used conventionally in epic and elsewhere to introduce a narrative.

44 **the case of the ass on the roof-tops**. This is probably a proverbial saying indicating that something is extraordinary.

45 **the inimitable Apelles**. A famous tragic actor in the reign of Caligula.

46 **Scylax**. It is amusing that Trimalchio's enormous dog has a Greek name meaning 'puppy'. Croesus' dog is appropriately named Margarita, 'Pearl'.

47 **'Hey cockalorum, how many are we?'** We should visualise a game, probably along the lines of the 'guess-how-many-fingers' game played earlier on (see note 25 on p. 139).

48 **Habinnas from the Priests' College**. See note 12 on p. 137. Apart from any similarities between Habinnas' entrance at Trimalchio's dining-room and the appearance of Alcibiades in Plato's *Symposium*, it is important to remember that Habinnas' description, his words, and his actions characterise him as a first-class parasite who shares most of the vulgar interests of his host.

49 **whoa, Palamedes!** The origin and meaning of this phrase (if, indeed, this is the correct manuscript reading) are unknown. Palamedes was a Greek warrior who died unjustly during the Trojan war.

50 **made out of the thousandth parts I owe Mercury**. Mercury was the patron-saint of merchants (he appears on the mural outside Trimalchio's house, and the host himself mentions him explicitly on p. 57 as his patron-deity); they in turn donated a small share of their profits to him. Since Trimalchio's bracelet is 'weighing not a fraction under ten pounds' (Trimalchio's boastful remark on p. 49), he must be earning at least ten thousand pounds of gold per month.

51 **I could be satisfied with this course, for you have had your second service.** Another of Trimalchio's childish puns; this time the host plays with the literal and the figurative meaning of the Latin phrase *secundae mensae* (= 'dessert' and 'second set of tables').

52 **Now Aeneas and his fleet had put to sea.** Virgil, *Aeneid*, V, 1.

53 **dirty Atellane verses.** Only fragments survive of the literary *fabula Atellana* of the first century BC. It was a form of native Italian theatrical entertainment with stock characters, farcical brief plots, and indecent jokes.

54 **The Muleteer's Life.** Probably the title of an obscene farcical sketch. In fact, this topic is one of the highlights in the slave's repertoire: 'Nobody can touch him when it comes to imitating mule-drivers . . . ' (Habinnas' words on p. 50).

55 **Daedalus.** The skilful cook is appropriately named after the architect of the Labyrinth (see note 33 on p. 140).

56 **the Greens.** One of the four chariot teams (the other three being Reds, Whites, and Blues) which took part in the Circus races of the time.

57 **the tragedian Ephesus.** Presumably a tragic actor unknown to us.

58 **the songs of Menecrates.** Famous lyre-player during the reign of Nero.

59 **if I can extend my farms as far as Apulia.** An area in lower Southern Italy. Trimalchio's aim in life is to possess almost the whole of Southern Italy.

60 **Scaurus.** The implication is that only distinguished and high-class Romans would visit Trimalchio.

61 **'Pretend I'm dead,' he said.** Although Tacitus and Seneca describe real instances of such morbid scenes, which in certain respects are strikingly similar to Trimalchio's death scene, it is plausible that Trimalchio, who has conceived almost every part of his dinner as a theatrical entertainment, should also have staged his death according to the rules of the farcical drama of which he was so fond. We must not assume, therefore, that this scene is intended to be taken seriously in order to underline the psychological decline brought about in Trimalchio by his luxurious life.

CHAPTER FOUR

1 **the scene of a Theban duel**. Giton is rather fancifully comparing the 'brothers' (in the sexual sense) Encolpius and Ascyltus with the natural brothers Eteocles and Polynices, sons of Oedipus king of Thebes, who fought for the throne of Thebes and killed each other in a duel. Giton presumably stands for the kingdom of Thebes!

2 **Menelaus**. The assistant tutor of Agamemnon at the school of rhetoric. Some critics have seen in this sentence an indication of Menelaus' homoerotic desires towards Encolpius.

3 **white shoes**. Encolpius is wearing a type of unmanly Greek shoes (*phaecasia*), worn also by Trimalchio's wife Fortunata.

4 **Unhappy Tantalus!** The king of Phrygia, who disobeyed the commands of the gods and was severely punished in the Under-world with terrible thirst and hunger; whenever he attempted to drink water, it receded from his lips, and every time he tried to pluck any fruit, it avoided his grasp.

5 **Zeuxis . . . Protogenes . . . Apelles**. Each of those Greek painters was famous for a different reason: Zeuxis for his realism and attention to detail; the Rhodian Protogenes for accuracy in colour; and Apelles for the precise outlining of the figures he portrayed, and his use of simple colour-schemes.

6 **the shepherd-boy of Ida . . . Hylas . . . Apollo . . . with a new-born flower**. Encolpius is looking at paintings with (explicitly or implicitly) homosexual themes, and is immediately inclined to compare his situation to that of the beautiful Trojan Ganymede, who was abducted by Zeus in the guise of an eagle, or to that of Hylas, lover of Hercules, who while drawing water was dragged in by a water-nymph, or to that of the Spartan prince Hyacinthus, accidentally killed by Apollo, god of light, who had fallen in love with him; the flower of the same name is said to have grown from the young man's blood.

7 **more cruel than Lycurgus himself**. It is very difficult to decide whether Encolpius alludes here to the Spartan law-giver Lycurgus, famous for his severe but fair legislation, or to a character of this novel called Lycurgus, who must have appeared in a missing section of the text, or to both of them; other references to the latter Lycurgus suggest that Encolpius killed him and stole his valuables (see note 22 on p. 148).

8 **a white-headed old man.** Appropriately enough, it is only after this man has recited a hackneyed poem attacking the superiority of material possessions over arts, and a mediocre epic composition on the Sack of Troy, that his name is revealed to the audience of the novel: it is Eumolpus, 'Mr Sweet-Singer'.

9 **'I don't know . . . to good sense.'** Is this Eumolpus continuing his tirade, or Encolpius agreeing with his interlocutor?

10 **'I wish the man . . . pimps themselves.'** These lines must surely belong to Encolpius, who is referring to Ascyltus.

11 **Asia . . . Pergamum.** The Roman province of Asia comprised only a small part of the land which used to be Asia Minor. Pergamum, one of its richest cities, functions here as the setting of one of the two cynical and obscene Milesian Tales incorporated by Petronius into the flow of his text, the Tale of the Pergamene Boy (see also note 15 on p. 147).

12 **Democritus . . . Eudoxus . . . Chrysippus . . . Lysippus . . . Myron . . . Phidias.** Democritus, the Abderite philosopher (fifth century BC), is commonly held to be one of the founders of the 'atomic theory', the other being Leucippus. Eudoxus of Cnidus (c.390–340 BC) was an astronomer, geometer and philosopher. Chrysippus (c.280–207 BC) was regarded as the most important member of the Stoic philosophical school. Lysippus was a celebrated fourth century BC sculptor of realistic rather than idealised human figures. The best known surviving work of the equally renowned sculptor Myron (fifth century BC) is the 'Discus Thrower'. Phidias (fifth century BC) was the famous Athenian sculptor whose works included the chryselephantine Athena and the statue of Zeus at Olympia.

13 **Now the tenth harvest of the Trojan siege.** This improvised epic composition (in iambic, not dactylic metre) of the Sack of Troy, a brief version of the events recounted in Virgil's *Aeneid* II, 13–267, is most likely targeted at Neronian poetasters with Eumolpus' poetic skills, rather than at Virgil himself.

14 **Good for Ganymede!** See note 6 on p. 144.

15 **'They despise . . . nothing else.'** Presumably this is Eumolpus speaking against luxury, a vice to which he himself is not averse.

16 **just as Ulysses of old clung to the belly of a ram.** Having blinded the Cyclops, Odysseus (Ulysses) and his companions escaped from the monster's cave by clinging to the belly of the Cyclops' sheep (Homer, *Odyssey*, IX, 426 ff.).

17 'Always and everywhere . . . '. Eumolpus is speaking, according
to the manuscripts.

18 and boarded the ship. It is true that, despite the narrator's later
statement that '[Eumolpus] had reserved his own passage long ago'
(p. 78), the reason and indeed the preparations for this journey are
not explicitly mentioned in the surviving text; this omission,
however, should not suggest that these pieces of information were
included in missing sections of the text. Journeys by sea were
hardly an original or surprising element in the novelistic tradition
which Petronius was following.

CHAPTER FIVE

1 Lichas of Tarentum . . . carrying Tryphaena to exile. Both
Lichas ('Mr Savage') and Tryphaena ('Ms Luxury') have appeared
in missing episodes of the text and have been in some way
wronged by Encolpius: he stole the handsome slave Giton from
Tryphaena and seduced Lichas' wife Hedyle. (See p. 82: 'Lichas
had not forgotten the seduction of his wife and the insult offered
him in Hercules' Walk'.) It is not made clear why Tryphaena is
going into exile. The sentence, 'Had she not been as heavily
wronged as Lichas, had not her reputation for modesty been
flouted in public?' (p. 81) suggests that her banishment may be a
punishment for her immoral behaviour. The reappearance of these
characters enables Petronius to play with the motif of Fortune and
its power over the hero of the novel, and to parody superstitious
beliefs .

2 What new Hannibal. Lichas is jokingly compared to the cruel
and cunning Carthaginian general Hannibal, who posed a real
threat to Republican Rome and was eventually defeated in 202 BC.
Ironically enough, Lichas will actually be a threat to Encolpius'
and Giton's lives.

3 Cover them, and everyone will offer his arm to the sick!
Headgear other than helmets would suggest to a Roman either
effeminacy or illness.

4 Just because the trick came off once on a notorious occasion?
Encolpius is possibly referring to Cleopatra's extraordinary idea to
wrap herself up in a carpet and thus have herself carried secretly to
Caesar.

5 **I thought I heard**. Lichas is speaking.

6 **Priapus**. See note 5 on p. 135.

7 **Epicurus**. Celebrated Greek moral and natural philosopher (341–270 BC) and founder of the Epicurean philosophical sect, which praised freedom from pain as the highest good, defined pleasure as the aim in life (see p. 114), and explained phenomena such as dreams in a rationalistic way. It is highly ironical, of course, that the double dream of Lichas and Tryphaena is not to be explained away as a reflection of their desires, but actually foreshadows events which will happen in the same episode.

8 **with Spartan composure**. The ability to endure physical pain was regarded by the Spartans as a great virtue.

9 **Ulysses' nurse**. It was a scar on the leg of Odysseus (Ulysses) that revealed his true identity to his aged nurse Euryclea (Homer, *Odyssey*, XIX, 467 ff.); in this farcical scene Lichas, the equivalent of the nurse, recognises his enemy Encolpius, the comic Odysseus, not by a scar or a similar wound but by his penis.

10 **the seduction of his wife**. See note 1 on p. 146.

11 **Had she not been as heavily wronged as Lichas**. See note 1 on p. 146.

12 **I believe they have chosen me**. Eumolpus is intervening to help his friends.

13 **What salamander has scorched your eyebrows?** Lichas is here addressing Encolpius. The belief was that contact with a salamander, a type of lizard, resulted in total loss of hair.

14 **no Trojan hero . . . a raging Medea**. The Trojan prince Paris stole Helen from her husband, king Menelaus of Sparta, and this was said to have caused the Trojan War. Medea helped Jason to take the golden fleece, then fled with him and her brother Apsyrtus from Colchis; to delay her family who were chasing them, she is said to have mutilated her brother and thrown his body to her pursuers.

15 **There was a married woman of Ephesus**. This is a masterfully told story. Its brevity, its brisk narrative pace, its unexpected ending, and the cynical way in which literary allusions are incorporated in its plot have rightly made the Milesian Tale of the Widow of Ephesus (a wealthy city on the south-west coast of modern Turkey) perhaps the most celebrated section of the novel.

16 'Will you fight against a love that pleases?' With these words
    Anna attempted to console her grief-stricken sister, a more famous
    widow, Dido (Virgil, *Aeneid*, IV, 38).

17 Hedyle . . . pleasure-cruise. Presumably Hedyle ('Mrs Sweetie')
    was Lichas' spouse, seduced by Encolpius. The exact events on
    Lichas' ship cannot be reconstructed with certainty. (See note 20.)

18 He tried to cut in. Presumably Lichas.

19 If you had a drop of good blood in you. According to the
    manuscripts, the speaker is the 'maid of Tryphaena addressing
    Encolpius'.

20 Give the ship back her sacred robe and rattle. Are these sacred
    items, traditionally regarded as the emblems of the Egyptian
    goddess Isis, the loot which Encolpius took when he seduced
    Hedyle? (See note 17 above.)

21 Croton, a town of high antiquity. Originally a celebrated Greek
    colony, Croton became Roman in 194 BC, but by Petronius' time
    it had long lost its splendour. It is appropriate, therefore, that it is
    used as the morally degenerate setting for the amorous adventures
    of Encolpius and Circe, and the legacy-hunting schemes of
    Eumolpus.

22 whatever we found in Lycurgus' villa when we broke in. This
    episode does not survive. (See note 7 on p. 144.)

23 the mother of the gods. The Eastern goddess Cybele.

24 he has scaled Helicon. Mount Helicon in Boeotia was sacred to
    Apollo, god of light and poetry, and to the Muses.

25 'I hate the common mob, and hold it off.' The phrase appears in
    inverted commas because it is a quotation from Horace, *Odes*, III,
    1, 1.

26 Now the whole world was the Roman conqueror's. This
    intolerably long epic poem on the hackneyed theme of the Civil
    War between Caesar and Pompey (the latter was defeated by the
    former in the battle at Pharsalus in Thessaly at 48 BC) may have
    been the poem Eumolpus was composing during the shipwreck
    (see p. 92), and is perhaps best regarded as a literary product whose
    artistic value should not exceed the mediocre poetic talent of its
    author. Its inclusion in the narrative creates problems for the
    generic classification of Petronius' text, and its narrative function
    remains for many scholars an open question. As with Eumolpus'

previous lengthy composition on the Sack of Troy (see pp. 66–68),
I have refrained from adding historical notes at this point. The
interested reader will find those in the works cited on p. xvii,
'Other Modern Translations'.

CHAPTER SIX

1 **What if Eumolpus' man**. Presumably, this is Corax ('the crow');
some critics have actually suggested that Encolpius' fears do mater-
ialise in a later, missing episode of the novel: Corax, the loquacious
crow, will be responsible for the betrayal of Eumolpus' secret to
the Crotonians.

2 **When you say you are a low slave**. Encolpius Polyaenus is, of
course, only pretending to be Eumolpus' slave.

3 **she skips the fourteen rows from the orchestra**. The fourteen
rows in the theatre immediately behind the Senators had been
allotted, since 67 BC, to the wealthy class of the cavalrymen
(*equites*). Circe, therefore, is interested only in the lower classes.

4 **Praxiteles conceived for Diana**. Praxiteles was a celebrated
fourth century BC sculptor, who had made more than one statue of
Artemis, the Greek equivalent of the Roman goddess Diana.

5 **the marble of Paros**. Famous for its whiteness; the comparison is
hardly original.

6 **my ancient love for Doris**. Presumably she was Encolpius'
girlfriend right at the beginning of the (now lost) text. Circe is the
first woman in the surviving text for whom Encolpius clearly
expresses a sexual interest.

7 **to sprout horns . . . in swansdown . . . true Danaë**. The allusions are to Jupiter's transformations to a bull, a swan and a shower
of gold, to seduce Europa, Leda and Danaë, respectively.

8 **a sister**. In the sexual sense; see also note 11 on p. 134.

9 **the song of the Sirens**. See note 9 on p. 134.

10 **Circe loves Polyaenus with good reason**. Petronius is playing
with the Homeric Circe, daughter of the Sun and a sorceress who
turned Odysseus's companions into pigs, and with Odysseus, who
is frequently given the epithet *poluaenos* (πολύαινος) 'much
praised', in the *Odyssey*. The seductive witch becomes in the
Satyricon a nymphomaniac aristocratic lady, who fails twice to
arouse her comically impotent Odysseus.

11 **What is it?' she said.** This is Circe speaking, presumably referring to Encolpius' inability to perform sexually.

12 **Alcibiades in his master's bed.** An ironical reference to the allegedly 'platonic' love between Socrates and his beautiful pupil, the politician and general Alcibiades (Plato, *Symposium*, 217–19).

13 **that made an Achilles of me.** The almost invincible hero in Homer's *Iliad* could boast of homosexual as well as heterosexual liaisons.

14 **a little old woman trailing behind.** This is Proselenus ('Ms Older-than-the-Moon'), a comic hag employed, presumably by Circe, to cure Encolpius' impotence.

15 **The lady was exasperated.** In spite of the success of Proselenus' magic tricks, Encolpius again fails to make love to Circe.

16 **He went on looking at the ground.** Encolpius' risible conversation with his penis becomes even more comic when the penis responds in exactly the same way as Dido, when Aeneas attempted to approach her ghost in the Underworld (Virgil, *Aeneid*, VI, 469).

17 **Catos of this age.** Marcus Porcius Cato, censor in 184 BC, was a byword for puritanical attitudes to moral issues.

18 **wise Epicurus.** See note 7 on p. 147.

19 **Friend of the nymphs.** Encolpius addresses his prayer to the phallic god Priapus, whose parents were Dionysus (Bacchus) and Aphrodite (Dione was her mother's name, which was used in poetry also for her). Presumably the narrative gap preceding the prayer must have contained Encolpius' decision to visit the Priapic shrine.

20 **an old woman.** This is Proselenus; it is she who is addressing Encolpius in the following paragraph.

21 **Then the priestess came in.** Another priestess of Priapus; she is called Oenothea ('Goddess-of-Wine'), and is portrayed as bibulous and comically amorous in the tradition of Roman elegiac hags with magic powers.

22 **Proteus.** A water-deity, who to escape from his pursuers, had the ability to transform himself into any shape he wished to take.

23 **Ceres.** The Roman counterpart to Demeter, the Greek goddess of vegetation.

24 **Hecale of old ... Callimachus the poet.** The famous Alexandrian poet and scholar Callimachus wrote an influential

epic poem, which does not survive, on the generous hospitality the poor and old Hecale provided to the legendary king Theseus after he killed the Cretan bull.

25 **the birds of Stymphalus . . . the Harpies**. The farcical quality of Encolpius' mock-epic battle with Oenothea's geese is enhanced by the comparison of the domestic birds with the mythological creatures which plagued lake Stymphalus in Arcadia but were eventually frightened away by Hercules, and with the Harpies, again enormous birds, which punished the Thracian king Phineus by preventing him from eating and drinking; they were driven away by two of the Argonauts.

26 **Here are two gold pieces**. Is this part of the loot from Lycurgus' country house (see p. 94, 'whatever we found in Lycurgus' villa when we broke in'), or a share of the money the Crotonians have been showering on Eumolpus (see p. 105, 'All the legacy-hunters solicited Eumolpus' favour with presents')?

27 **Servius and Labeo**. Eminent lawyers, the former of the Ciceronian period, the latter of the Augustan age.

28 **'Ariadne or Leda'**. After the comic escape of Encolpius from the hopeless clutches of the two drunken hags, the hero appears to be visited by Circe's maid Chrysis, who confesses that her feelings towards him have changed (is this a genuine change?); Encolpius, however, is still obsessed with Circe. Ready to forgive and forget, he compares her to the legendary beauties (notice the climactic order of names) Ariadne, Leda, Helen and Venus.

29 **Laomedon . . . Pelias . . . Telephus . . . Nereus**. Laomedon, king of Troy, was helped by Poseidon and Apollo to build the city walls, but incurred their wrath because he refused to pay them the promised reward. Pelias, son of Poseidon and Tyro, and responsible for the expedition of the Argonauts in search of the Golden Fleece, neglected to honour Hera (Juno). The allusion to Telephus, an Arcadian hero, son of Hercules and Auge, is obscure. Nereus was a water-deity and the father of the Nereids, water-nymphs.

30 **a woman came in**. This is probably Circe.

31 **our master was most furious**. The servant refers to Eumolpus, the alleged master of Encolpius, Giton and Corax.

32 **to make a sacrifice to Venus Callipyge**. Although the Latin is corrupt here, an act of sodomy between the old man and the girl is probably the meaning of this euphemism.

33 **but here too I came up against my hostile deity**. Although the hero seems to be sexually unsuccessful even with Philomela's son, he will very soon regain his virility with the help of Mercury, god of thieves and guide of souls on the way to the Underworld. It is not clear why the god restores Encolpius' virility at this point in the narrative and not earlier.

34 **Socrates, beloved of men and gods**. Presumably this is Eumolpus engaged in conversation with Encolpius. The context of the discussion is very vague.

35 **The ship you promised from Africa**. Eumolpus is addressed probably by Encolpius (note the latter's obsession with the power of Fortune).

36 **that they cut my body to pieces and eat it in public**. In order to get rid of his ruthless heirs, Eumolpus is setting them this revolting task; however, the Crotonians do not seem discouraged by this clause of Eumolpus' will.

WORDSWORTH CLASSICS
OF WORLD LITERATURE

APULEIUS
The Golden Ass

LODOVICO ARIOSTO
Orlando Furioso

ARISTOTLE
The Nicomachean Ethics

MARCUS AURELIUS
Meditations

FRANCIS BACON
Essays

JEREMY BENTHAM
Utilitarianism

JAMES BOSWELL
The Life of Samuel Johnson
(UNABRIDGED)

JOHN BUNYAN
The Pilgrim's Progress

BALDASSARE CASTIGLIONE
The Book of the Courtier

CATULLUS
Poems

CERVANTES
Don Quixote

CARL VON CLAUSEWITZ
On War
(ABRIDGED)

CONFUCIUS
The Analects

CAPTAIN JAMES COOK
The Voyages of Captain Cook

DANTE
The Inferno

CHARLES DARWIN
The Origin of Species
The Voyage of the Beagle

RENÉ DESCARTES
Key Philosophical Writings

DOSTOEVSKY
The Brothers Karamazov

ERASMUS
Praise of Folly

SIGMUND FREUD
The Interpretation of Dreams

EDWARD GIBBON
*The Decline and Fall of the
Roman Empire*
(ABRIDGED)

KAHLIL GIBRAN
The Prophet

JOHAN WOLFGANG
VON GOETHE
Faust

HERODOTUS
Histories

THOMAS HOBBES
Leviathan

HOMER
The Iliad
The Odyssey

HORACE
The Odes

KENKO
Essays in Idleness

WILLIAM LANGLAND
Piers Plowman

T. E. LAWRENCE
Seven Pillars of Wisdom

JOHN LOCKE
*Essay Concerning Human
Understanding*
(ABRIDGED)

NICCOLÒ MACHIAVELLI
The Prince

SIR THOMAS MALORY
Le Morte Darthur

JOHN STUART MILL
*On Liberty & The Subjection
of Women*

SIR THOMAS MORE
Utopia

FRIEDRICH NIETZSCHE
Thus Spake Zarathustra

OVID
Metamorphoses

*Ars Amatoria, Amores
and Remedia Amoris*

THOMAS PAINE
Rights of Man

SAMUEL PEPYS
The Concise Pepys

PETRONIUS
Satyricon

PLATO
Republic

*Symposium and
the Death of Socrates*

PLUTARCH
Lives
(SELECTED)

MARCO POLO
The Travels

FRANÇOIS RABELAIS
Gargantua and Pantagruel

JEAN RACINE
Three Plays

LA ROCHEFOUCAULD
Maxims

JEAN-JACQUES ROUSSEAU
The Confessions

The Social Contract

WILLIAM SHAKESPEARE
Four Great Comedies

Five Great Tragedies

Five Great History Plays

Five Classical Plays

Four Late Plays

EDMUND SPENSER
The Faerie Queene

SPINOZA
Ethics

SUETONIUS
Lives of the Twelve Caesars

LAO TZU
Tao te ching

THUCYDIDES
*The History of the
Peloponnesian War*

ALEXIS DE TOCQUEVILLE
Democracy in America
(ABRIDGED)

SUN TZU
*The Art of War
(with The Book of
Lord Shang)*

VIRGIL
The Aeneid

Five Jacobean Tragedies

Four Restoration Comedies

The Koran

The Newgate Calendar

Njal's Saga

*Sir Gawain and
the Green Knight*

The Upanishads